DANGEROUS TURNS

THE UNPUBLISHED MYSTERIES OF
PETER PAIGE

Encyclopocalypse Publications
www.encyclopocalypse.com

An Encyclopocalypse Book

Cover design by Amanda Dempsey.

Edited by Mike Watt.

Interior layout and design by Mark Alan Miller.

First Edition 2026.

Printed in the United States of America.

ISBN: 978-19660376-06

DANGEROUS TURNS

THE UNPUBLISHED MYSTERIES OF
PETER PAIGE

contents

the facks of life

THE DAY STARTED lousy because I woke up too early and went to see if mom was up yet. She was up all right. But when I opened her door I forgot all about asking her to give me breakfast. She was wrestling pop. He was on top and it looked like he was killing her. I got so mad I grabbed one of his shoes off the floor and banged his head with it.

His hand felt like a baseball bat on my mouth. I landed against the bureau across the room and mom was yelling at me. At *me*! And pop was talking through his teeth in that quiet way that's worse than yelling, telling me to get out of there and get out of there fast.

I got out all right. I didn't feel hungry no more. I felt sick enough to puke almost. I didn't wash or brush my teeth, or anything. I dressed so fast I put on different colored socks, and when I ran out of the apartment I slammed the door so hard I bet I damn near woke up everybody in the whole apartment house.

I was so mixed up I didn't watch where I was going and before I knew it I was passing Murphy's Palace. It's on the corner a block from school and the kids go there for candy and ice cream and stuff. I used to go there until old man Murphy caught me begging Carmine to stop buying them crazy cigarettes there.

I didn't like how they made him act like he was drunk or something. I mean Carmine Hernandez, my best friend. He's sixteen and still only in my class, but not because he's dumb. He's going to be a dancer on the stage and TV and movies and make a lot of money, so why should he knock his brains out over school?

Anyhow, since he started smoking he was acting real creepy. He'd been borrowing my lunch money for two whole weeks and never paid back a cent. And then he didn't come out on the street to play stick-ball no more. And he didn't take me down the basement where his people is janitors and practice new steps, with me banging a stick on a pail like a drummer in a band.

All he could talk about was girls. Not regular girls like Heather or Laurie in class, or like that. Old women like that Olga he once showed me. She's at least twenty. When he'd be smoking those stinking cigarettes he'd say, "She's got what I need, Tommy, and one of these days I'm gonna get it."

"What's she got that's so special?" I asked him, and he wiggled his hands and said, "These and those, kid," and I thought he meant her behind, which was so fat it bounced when she walked and I thought that was disgusting.

So I was telling him not to get any more of those crazy cigarettes and he was telling me he'd go crazy if he didn't have a smoke quick and we got pretty loud and old man Murphy stuck his head out the door and asked Carmine, "Who's that?"

Carmine told him, "My friend, Tommy Brighton," and old man Murphy got red in the face.

He said, "Anything to do with Captain Brighton down the Precinct?"

"That's his pop," Carmine told him.

And old man Murphy said, "Beat it!"

Carmine winked and said, "I got half a buck for a smoke!"

Old man Murphy looked like he was going to choke. He yelled, "I don't sell cigarettes to kids!"

Carmine said, "I don't mean cigarettes."

"You want to get me in trouble?" old man Murphy yelled at him. "Beat it! Both of you!"

Carmine kept trying to beg him, but old man Murphy went in back and came out with a fungo bat and we ran like hell.

That was two days ago. I'd been staying away from Murphy's Palace, but this morning I was so mixed up I didn't watch where I was going. I was going to school, but it wouldn't open for two hours yet, but I was going that way anyhow, thinking maybe I'd run away or something. Sure, my pop spanked me before—but never with his hand on my face. And my mom never yelled at me. Never in my whole life.

So I didn't notice where I was until someone grabbed me from behind and picked me up in the air and I found out where I was going. Straight into Murphy's Palace!

A fat man was sitting in a booth with a man with a mustache. They had been eating breakfast, and when the fat man saw me being carried in, he said, "What the hell's going on?"

From right behind me I heard old man Murphy say, "It's the Brighton kid I was telling you about. He'd know where to find—" and he stopped talking, because the fat man jumped up looking mad.

It gave me the creeps how the fat man looked. Even though he was dressed pretty fancy for this part of the Bronx, Everything was grey except his tie. That was black. Even his hat was grey. The fat on his cheeks came up so high it almost closed his eyes. They was like slits. He talked quiet—but even that was scary. He said, "Put the kid down."

I went down so fast I landed on my hands and knees. When I got up and looked around old man Murphy was so red, like his face was on fire. He kept opening and closing his mouth, but no words came out. The fat man laughed and I looked at him. He winked. "You scared of Murph, Kid?"

All I could think to say was, "He chased me and Carmine with a fungo bat."

"Yeah? Why?"

I said, "He wouldn't let Carmine buy those crazy cigarettes here."

"That's real bright," the fat man told old man Murphy.

All of a sudden the other man in the booth laughed. "Murph's a genius," he said. This was a little man. He had a little black mustache and his face was kind of yellow and his teeth were all crooked when he laughed. But his eyes didn't laugh at all. They just looked at old man Murphy. Old man Murphy was sweating.

"Get the bat," the fat man told him.

Old man Murphy just stood there sweating, and the other man stopped laughing. He yelled, "Now!"

Old man Murphy jumped. He ran in back and came out with the fungo bat.

"Give it to the kid," the fat man said.

I took the bat. I was scared.

"Don't move," the fat man told old man Murphy. "Don't move one little inch." Then he laughed and patted my shoulder and said, "Go ahead, Kid. Bop him one."

I was so scared I wet my pants a little. I could hardly hold onto the bat. I looked at the fat man and shook my head. I was afraid if I talked I'd start bawling.

But he just patted my shoulder and took the bat from me and told old man Murphy, "It's your lucky day, Brainwave. Set up a breakfast for the kid. Whatever he wants." Then he pushed me into the booth and he sat down opposite me next to the man with the mustache and said, "You don't look that school-happy, Kid, coming so early. I bet you had an argument at home and walked out without breakfast, hey?"

It was like he could read my mind. I said that was right and he said it happened to him a lot when he was a kid, and I wasn't so scared any more. And then when old man Murphy began bringing me stuff like orange juice and bacon and eggs and a chocolate malted, with the man with the mustache saying funny things like, "Move, Brainwave!" and, "Get the lead out, Einstein!" and stuff like that I couldn't help laughing.

Pretty soon I was talking with the fat man just like he was 'nother feller and I was telling him about me and Carmine. "That's the redheaded kid, hey?" the fat man asked. "Always wearing a T-shirt with 'Yankees' on it, hey?"

I told him Carmine had black hair and he only wore Mets T-shirts and the fat man winked at his friend and I knew he'd been kidding me. Then asked me why Carmine didn't come to school the last few days and my throat got so tight I could hardly get the malted down.

Because when old man Murphy chased us, Carmine yelled at me, "You loused me up!" I asked him, "For crying out loud, how? There's a million places you can buy cigarettes if you want them so crazy." But he just kept talking to himself, saying, "What'll I do? What'll I do? *Dios mio*, I'll go nuts!" Then he started walking away as if he forgot I was there. But he knew, all right. When I started after him, I got the back of his hand in my face. When I got home my mom asked me who I fought and I said see the other guy and she laughed. I almost bawled. And now I hadn't seen the other guy for two whole days.

I told the fat man, "I guess Carmine thinks it's my fault Mr. Murphy won't sell him cigarettes."

"Genius!" the man with the mustache said.

Old man Murphy kept sweating.

The fat man said, "I don't like to see kids shoved around. How's for finding Carmine and bringing him here so I'll fix it he can get all the smokes he wants, hey?"

"I don't know where he is."

"You'd know where to look for him better than anyone else, hey?"

"Well, sure," I told him. "I'm his best friend. But he isn't in the neighborhood and the other places he goes is too far for me to go alone."

The fat man laughed. "You wouldn't be alone if we came along. After school, hey? You have to go right home after school?"

I started to say yes, but then I remembered how my mom yelled at me when I was only trying to protect her. I said I didn't, and the fat man said, "Okay, that's it. After school Joey, here, and me'll be parked around the corner. We'll show you the car so you won't miss it."

Then he made old man Murphy give me some candy bars and we walked a couple of blocks and his car turned out to be a brand new green Cadillac, and it was so smooth-looking it made me feel all funny inside just seeing it. I got all choked up, asking, "Will I get to ride in it?"

He laughed and said we sure as hell would and I was so excited I forgot all about having to go to the toilet until the middle of Mrs. Appell's class. It made her sore, but I didn't care.

Carmine wasn't in class again and I didn't care about that either. Sure I wanted to straighten everything out between us. But if he'd of showed up I wouldn't get that ride.

After lunch, in Arithmetic, when Miss Noslow told me to report to the Principal's office, I thought it was because of the spitball fight I'd had with Willie Fox, but when I got to Mr. Washington's office the first thing I saw was my pop.

Carmine's mom and pop were there also. They're Puerto Ricans. They don't talk American good. They're little, with sort of wrinkled faces and they looked scared, like I felt inside. Not my pop, though. He never looks scared. He looked like he did when he told me to get out of mom's room and stay out. And he talked the same way. Through his teeth.

"Tommy, when's the last time you saw Carmine?"

I talked back through my teeth, kind of looking at the floor. Told him two days ago. He asked where. I said around the block. Mr. Washington said, "Captain, the idea is ridiculous."

"Sure," my pop said. He sounded tired. "So is Greasy Burke. He belongs back in the Twenties, along with Dutch Schultz and Legs Diamond. But he sure scared hell out of Mr. and Mrs. Hernandez last night. Why do you think he wants Carmine? To help him with his homework?"

"Not that," Mr. Washington said. "The idea of narcotics being used by our Elementary School children—"

"Sure!" my pop said through his teeth. "Tell me we didn't break up a gang rumble in Claremont Park last night. Four of the kids were from this school, two of 'em high on reefers. Greasy Burke wouldn't be interested in that kind of peanuts except as a minor sideline—not enough to visit the Hernandez' personally—" My pop stopped talking to look at me. He said, "You sure, Tommy?"

I looked down at the floor and nodded. Mrs. Hernandez said, "*Par favor,* Tomas. Eef you see Carmine, tell him come home."

I said I'd look for him after school and she put her arm around me and said I was a good boy, and Mr. Hernandez shook hands with me just like I was growed up, and then I had to go back to class. But I was too worried to learn anything. If my pop found Carmine first I'd miss a ride in the green Cadillac.

That talk about Greasy Burke went over my head. My pop is always talking about him, and I'd heard so much 'Greasy Burke this' and 'Greasy Burke that' my ears kind of closed when he got mentioned. When I once asked my pop why he didn't arrest him if he was such a bad guy my pop got sore and mom changed the subject.

But I guessed my pop hadn't found Carmine yet when I hit the street after school. That green Cadillac was still there, with Joey in it. He told me to get in and hunker low so the other kids wouldn't see me and bug him for a ride, so I did. I could feel us moving, and when we stopped the fat man got in the back. He laughed at me and said I could sit up. I saw we were on Tremont. A big man with a bent nose got in after the fat man. Joey looked sideways at me. "Where to, Kid?"

I said movies, because Carmine likes to sit next to older girls in the balcony and grab feels. The fat man asked what movies and I told him, and the next hour I never saw so little of so many pictures in my whole life, even in the Paradise, up on the Concourse. I saw a lot of disgusting stuff in the balconies. But no Carmine.

After a while the fat man said, "Let's get off this movie kick, Kid. Where else?"

I said dance halls, but it was too early for that. Then I remembered once before Carmine stayed out all night, and when I said that the fat man got all excited.

So I told him how Carmine got talking about old Olga one afternoon when he was smoking those cigarettes. That was the night he didn't come home. When I asked him about it next day, he said he'd gone to the roof of the house across from Olga's to catch peeks. He said he saw plenty, but just when she was going to bed she pulled down her window shade —but not all the way down. So he went down to the street and around the block and up to the roof of her building and climbed down the fire escape and looked under the shade and saw she was in bed, but the covers were off and she wasn't wearing nothing and she was smoking one of those crazy cigarettes. Without thinking, he said, "How's for lighting one up for me?" Then he got scared because she heard him. Her bed was right next to the window. But when she looked to see who talked to her she didn't get mad or anything. She opened the window all the way for him, and that's where he was the whole night.

"Olga who?" asked the fat man. I told him, "He showed her to me once. She's got black hair and a fat behind." Joey laughed. "Great! All we gotta do is check out every fat-assed brunette in the Bronx!"

"Not the whole Bronx," I said. "Carmine showed me the house on Webster Avenue where he went up to the roof and got his peeks."

The fat man patted my shoulder from the back seat. He said, "I knew you were a smart kid the minute I laid eyes on you. Let's go!"

Gee, that Cadillac went smooth! It was so great, I felt like saying I wasn't sure which house, so we could keep riding, but my pop tanned the lying out of me when I was a little kid, so I showed them the house, and the fat man and the big man with the broken nose and me climbed six floors to the roof.

From there we could look down into the windows of two houses, one across the alley and one sideways, but I didn't know which one had Olga. The fat man walked back and forth awhile, then he asked me, "Did Carmine tell you what he saw when he looked in the window?"

I got red telling him. I mean the top of her bathroom window was open a little and he could see her back when she sat on the toilet and then all of her when she took a shower. And through the window at the fire escape he could see almost the whole room before she pulled the shade down.

"That narrows it to the top floor of the building across the alley, Rocky," the fat man told the big man with the broken nose. "That narrows it down to those four windows, two on each fire escape."

Rocky said, "That one, Boss."

He was pointing to a window with the shade all the way down except for a few inches at the bottom.

The fat man winked at me. "I bet that's it, Kid. I bet if you go downstairs and go around the block and up to the roof of that house and shinny down the ladder to that fire escape and peek in that window You'll see Carmine, hey?"

I asked, "Wouldn't be easier just to go to that apartment's door and ring the bell?"

"Maybe," the fat man said. "But would Carmine answer the bell? He might think old Murph was after him, hey? But if you talked to him from the fire escape and you told him it was all fixed up, he'd go home with you, wouldn't he? And we'd be waiting right outside the door, ready to drive you both home in the Caddy, hey?"

That made sense, so the three of us went down to the street, around the block and up the stairs of the other house. The fat man and Rocky waited outside what we figured was the apartment door while I went up to the roof.

Climbing down the ladder to the top-floor fire escape was easy. But slipping past the first window without being seen was another story. A fat lady inside was shaving herself. Honest to God, she was all bent over on a bed and shaving her leg with an electric razor. There was little metal things in her hair and brown stuff all over her face. Then she looked up and saw me and screamed and I backed off so quick I almost fell off of the fire escape.

But I forgot all about her when I peeked under the shade of the other window where the fat man said I would see Carmine. I saw Carmine, all right. And old Olga. They was wrestling. Honest to God, it made me feel so crawly inside I thought I would choke up or something.

I mean they was wrestling like mom and pop that morning, only a little different. At first I thought Carmine was winning, because he was on top. But how she was wrapped around him he could hardly move. He moved so slow it was like he was dying or something. And then she bit into his neck so hard, blood came.

It scared me so much, I yelled.

Their faces came around and Carmine gave me a dopey grin. I mean blood was on his neck and everything and he grinned like it was nothing and said, "Hi, Tommy." And old Olga said, "Holy Mother of God, what is it?"

Carmine said, "It's my friend Tommy."

Olga kind of pushed him off her and said, "I want some ice cream. "

"I give you the world, Baby," Carmine told her.

But he stayed on the bed and his eyes closed like he was falling asleep. Olga looked at me—but not really looking at me, just looking in my direction like she was daydreaming. And she said, "Don't just stand there with your head in the window, big eyes. The spic's on a cloud, but you could get me ice cream, huh? Chocolate. I could eat a gallon!"

I was all mixed up inside. I mean, they looked so groggy, and the air smelled so bad inside, I started to pull my head back to smell good air again but all of a sudden old Olga had grabbed hold of me and pulled me right into the room right on top of her. I almost puked in the time it took to break her grip and crawl over both of them to the floor.

Carmine didn't even seem to notice. And old Olga said, "If you don't wanna play, up yours!" And she rolled toward the window like she was going to sleep.

It was like I was in the middle of a nightmare or something. The room looked like nobody cleaned it in a year.

Everything was just chucked around and stepped on. And the smell was awful.

Even touching Carmine's shoulder to wake him up made me feel crawly. It was all sweaty. I shook it and he mumbled something and I shook it harder and he pushed my hand away and sat up. He had a hard time fixing his eyes on me. When he did, he sort of giggled and said, "Hi, Tommy."

I told him, "Your mom and pop are looking for you."

He said, "Tell 'em I'm riding high." Even when he smoked those crazy cigarettes he never talked that creepy.

I said, "Old Man Murphy'll sell you cigarettes again. And a guy I know will give you all you want free. "

"Muggles," Carmine said.

I said, "Those crazy cigarettes. You know."

He giggled, like a girl when she hears you say bastard or something. He said, "Muggles is for beginners, Tommy. I'm jagging high now. Me 'n Olga." He giggled again and slapped her fat behind. She was snoring. He said, "I guess you're learning the facks of life, hah, Tommy?"

I could hardly talk. All I could say was, "Don't you wanna come home with me, Carmine. We'll go in a Cadillac!"

He said, "Nah." And then he leaned over old Olga and what he did was so disgusting I felt like my insides were loose and crawling around.

I ran for the bathroom, but I didn't know where it was and got sick all over a blue rug. When my puking stopped, I knew I couldn't stand no more. I didn't care about Carmine or anything. I wanted to get out. I ran around until I found the front door. I opened it and Rocky jumped in and grabbed me.

Before I could yell his hand came over my mouth so tight it felt like my neck was going to break. I could see the fat man come in after him and close the door. He gave me the kind of look that made old man Murphy sweat. He whispered, "You sure took your goddamn time. They here?"

He wasn't really asking. He'd taken out a big black revolver from somewhere inside his jacket and he looked around. All he could see from there was the living room, where I'd puked. He said, "Which way, punk?"

Rocky's hand came away from my mouth. I took a big breath and yelled: "Carmine! Watch out!"

My head exploded.

Then I was laying on the floor. I didn't feel nothing. I was hearing somebody clap hands slow, like at a baseball game when the fans want to rattle the other team's pitcher. I listened to it awhile, then opened my eyes and found I was back in the bedroom.

Nobody was clapping hands. The fat man was slapping Carmine's face. Carmine was on his knees on the bed and blood was coming out of his nose and he had two black eyes and the fat man just held his head up by the hair and kept slapping Carmine's face with the front and back of his other hand. He was talking quiet, like the way he'd made old man Murphy sweat. He was saying, "Where is it, Greaseball? Where'd you stash it? Come on, talk up, you spic—" and then a lot of dirty names.

All of a sudden the door opened and Rocky dragged old Olga into the room. I could hear a shower running somewhere. Olga was all soaking wet, like she'd showered but hadn't dried off, and some of the wet was on Rocky's dark suit. She was fat in a lot of places and it was all wet and shaking. She looked scared half to death. Rocky laughed and said, "Olga don't wanna hold out no more, Boss."

Even Olga's voice was shaking. She said. "Honest to God, Mr. Burke, if I'd a knowed he stole it from you, I wouldn't a touched it!"

The fat man let Carmine go and Carmine just stayed on

his knees, with his head hanging down, like he'd fallen asleep while he was praying. The fat man said, "All I want to know is where it is. You two couldn't have shot it all, not even in two months, let alone two days. There was over half a million dollars worth of powder in those packages. Where are they?"

Olga said, "Honest to God, Mr. Burke, he just brung up a couple of decks. He—"

The fat man's fist moved so fast I didn't see it until Olga's head jerked back. When it came straight again, her mouth was all bloody. It was terrible, but I couldn't look away. The blood ran down and mixed with the wet. If Rocky didn't hold her tight she'd a caved in.

He hung onto her arm and her knees was bent and wobbling. And blood kept coming out of her mouth and the fat man suddenly yelled, "You want I should plant you in a five-buck-house in Harlem?"

All she could do was shake her head from side to side. Her eyes was rolling like they was loose. I thought the fat man was going to punch her again. But he went back to Carmine. He reached between Carmine's legs.

Carmine screamed like I once heard a cat when it was half run over by a truck. He fell over backwards. His head hit the shade and it snapped up and spun on its roller, and inside the room everything became bright and glary from the sun.

I couldn't stand no more. Honest to God, I felt if I stayed there another minute I'd die.

Nobody saw me stand up. Olga was hanging onto Rocky and shaking like crazy and he was rubbing his hands allover her. The fat man was standing on the bed next to Carmine reaching up for the shade to pull it down again.

I grabbed the seat of his pants and yanked so hard, if I didn't duck sideways he'd of crushed me to death. I heard him yell when he landed on the floor, but I paid him no attention. I was going over Carmine. I mean I was crawling right over him. I didn't care. I was bawling like a girl. I went out that window so fast my head banged the fire escape railing. It hurt like crazy and made me kinda groggy.

The next thing, I was kinda waking up and seeing the fat man coming out the window to me. I saw if I tried getting to the ladder going up to the roof he could a grabbed me, and behind me it was a five floor drop to the alley.

I was more scared of the fat man than I was of falling. I mean he looked terrible. He was breathing hard and his face was all red and his little eyes stuck to me like they was nailed to my face.

I scrambled over the rail and started walking on the outside of the fire escape to where the stairway going down was.

But he was outta the window before I could get there. He made a grab for me. I kinda jumped sideways. My foot slipped. And then I was hanging onto the bottom of the fire escape by only one hand.

I could see him look down on me with his mouth open. Then he looked all around. Then he looked back at me and laughed and said, "Come on, Tommy. I lost my head inside. Let's go down and take another ride in the Cadillac."

While he was talking, I got my other hand on the fire escape's bottom rail and tried to kick one foot up. I paid no attention to what he said.

I knew why he kept looking from side to side. All that screaming. Every woman in all those apartments around the alley must a had their heads out the windows and they was all screaming. I never heard so much noise in my whole life.

The fat man leaned over the top railing and grabbed the back of my sweater and pulled me up a little.

I didn't want to go up like that. I gripped the bars harder. He let go my sweater and leaned down and grabbed me under the arms and began pulling up real strong. My hands were getting sweaty and slipping a little.

He kept saying it was all a mistake and I should come up and he wouldn't hurt me. It was hard to hear him through all that screaming.

But I didn't believe him. I didn't believe him one little bit. He got me halfway up and I was so crazy desperate I grabbed that bottom rail with all my might and yanked myself down.

And that did it. I felt his hands come loose from under my arms. Something hard smashed into my back. I thought he was trying to knock me loose.

But when I looked up, the fat man wasn't on the fire escape no more.

Rocky was looking out from the window.

Not at me.

He was looking down through the slats in the fire escape floor. His face was kinda green. He looked up. But still not at me. At all those ladies with their heads outta their windows and screaming looked around also. All their mouths were open, and one old woman with white hair looked like she'd gone to sleep right across her windowsill.

When I looked back at Rocky the window was empty. Everything inside me was spinning around. I tried to pull myself up but my arms was too weak. All I could do was hang there with my feet swinging in the air and everything inside my head fuzzy.

I yelled for Carmine to help me. Then I heard something like firecrackers inside. The next thing, Sergeant Bernstein, from my pop's precinct, crawled out on the fire escape and pulled me up over the top railing.

The last thing I saw before I got too dizzy to keep my eyes open was when I looked down as Sergeant Bernstein was pulling me up. A lot of people was down below in the alley and in the middle of them lay the fat man and he looked strange. Instead of a head, it looked like he had a big red flower sticking out of his neck.

~

My pop parked our Chevvie near Crotona Park after he got me from the hospital and tried to explain everything. I mean he explained it all right, I just didn't get some of it. Something about a lot of herring, or something. It makes people like they was drunk, only worse. Olga found out how it was being sent to Greasy Burke. The fat man was Greasy Burke. Olga got Carmine to swipe the stuff. They was gonna sell it and get a lot of money. But instead of selling it, they kept using it themselves.

Not all of it. My pop said they found most of it in screwy hiding places like sugar bowls and salt shakers and places like that.

He said Carmine would go to a hospital for dopes, which sounded like a joke, but my pop never jokes. After that, Carmine would go to a school in the country until he was eighteen. Olga would go to jail. So would old man Murphy, on account he sold something called "Mary Warner." And so would Joey. But not Rocky. Those screaming women had called the precinct and when Rocky ran out of the apartment he tried to shoot Sergeant Bernstein, but he got shot dead instead.

I had a black eye and cuts and some other stuff, but the doctor said nothing really serious, and my pop said I was better than the whole department because I practically busted the Greasy Burke Mob singlehanded. He said that to the reporters and TV cameras, so I almost felt it wasn't such a lousy day after all.

But I was still mixed up. I told him, "I guess I got outta line this morning. I mean about you and mom wrestling and all. I thought it was for real. But then I saw Carmine and old Olga wrestling, and how they acted, it was like playing, even though it looked terrible. I mean well—I guess I'm mixed up."

Pop looked mixed-up also. I mean it was like he was laughing, but his eyes was wet. He put his arm around me and said, "In a way it's like playing, Tommy. Another way, it's pretty serious. And you're right about what Carmine and Olga were doing being different." He lit his pipe and smoked it awhile, and then he said, "Let's see, you're twelve now—"

"Going on thirteen!" I told him fast.

"Going on thirteen," he said. "Okay. I guess it's time I told you some pretty important things. Like what you bust in on this morning. And the difference between that and what went on between Carmine and Olga. And what to expect for yourself in the years to come..."

So he told me and, honest to God, I was never so surprised by anything before in my whole life.

I guess Carmine was right. I really was learning the facks of life.

she loved to kill

1

Alice Peterson

PRINTED on the face and scrawled on the back of a quarter of a million dollar check compensating her for the death of her husband, Roger Peterson, sixty-eight. Natural causes.

The check lay on my desk. It had been signed by the treasurer of Urban Indemnity. Across from me sat Tom Willson, one of Urban's brighter directors. On the frosted glass door behind him could be read backwards:

INVESTIGATIONS

Under that, in smaller gilt lettering:

William Hunt
Chief Investigator
Howdy.

"So?" I asked Tom, fingering the cancelled check. He said, "We programmed the computer to handwriting analysis and ran five years of benefit checks through it and came up with these," laying three more cancelled checks on my desk.

Made out in sums of ninety thousand, two hundred and eighty thousand and three hundred and seventy-five thousand, respective payments on the deaths of Henry Johnson, sixty-three, Michael Burns, fifty-eight, and Steven Pryor, sixty-nine. I flipped them over and read the endorsements: Alice Johnson, Alice Burns, Alice Pryor. Nor did I have to be a computer to recognize the identical handwriting on all three...

I flipped them again. They covered a span of thirty months. I whistled.

"Burns died of pneumonia," Tom said. "The others—'natural causes.'"

"Cremated?"

Tom shrugged. "All I know is Met has her on two checks, Mutual, on three. We're hit hardest, for almost a million. So they're putting it in our lap. The nine payments add up to a bit over two and half million. All in a space of roughly three years."

"Tax free!" I breathed reverently.

"Not to mention what she must have inherited. She probably has close to ten million by now. Handle it personally, Bill." I was already on my phone. A cigarette later, I listened to a long distance operator give way to a lazy drawl.

"Sheriff White. Tupelaca."

"Hunt. Urban Indemnity, of New York. A man in your county died last week. Roger Peterson."

"Buried Rog last Friday, Mistuh Hunt, is it?"

"Right... buried?"

"Yep."

"Sure he wasn't cremated?"

"Family plot. Ah was one o' the pallbearers."

"The widow still in Tupelaca?"

"Yep."

"Be seeing you."

"Suh?"

"I'm on my way."

~

What with getting to the plane, then off it, and the short cab ride, it was four hours before I sat across the office desk of Sheriff White in Tupelaca City, seat of Tupelaca County.

A deep-chested man in his forties, brown-haired and grey-eyed, he studied the facsimiles of the fronts and backs of the four checks, then me, then Doctor Bernstein, who I had borrowed from the New York Medical Examiner's office.

He clucked his tongue.

I waited.

He shook his head. "Ah'm sorry, Mistuh Hunt. Cain't order an exhumation without more'n this. Or the widder's consent. Four husbands who died ain't—"

"Nine," I interposed.

"Suh?"

"Other insurance companies are involved. Up to here, we know nine husbands died on her the past three years."

"Wal—" he reached into his khaki shirt and scratched. "Reckon Missus Alice got a taste for more mature men. She 'peared mighty fond o' old Rog. These checks—even nine of 'em—don't prove foul play. Might jus' be she had mis'able luck—"

Almost ten million dollars worth of mis'able luck. He was wasting my time. I parked Doc Bernstein in Tupelaca City's best hotel and grabbed a cab.

It left me before the shell-lined driveway of Spanish-type architecture. Red tile roofs and tawny walls. Only one floor high under towering Royal Palms, but sprawling in all directions. The lawn's mowing, as I negotiated the driveway, was at a hiatus.

A female drudge had abandoned the mower to chase a scrawny, big-eyed kid. He side-stepped her rushes neatly. She seemed to have too much bottom to move at his pace.

On second sight, not too much. What bottom she had seemed on the verge of coming through a raggedy grey dress. I watched them zigzag around the lawn awhile, then proceeded to a mahogany door featuring a brass knocker, which I knocked.

Nothing happened.

Behind me the chase continued. The woman finally began picking shells off the driveway's border and heaving them at him. Her aim was lousy.

She was panting when I appeared behind her and touched her shoulder.

I was still getting over my surprise at its softness when she turned to look at me.

A sullen face, tanned gold. Ordinary features. Lidded brown eyes, and brown hair as combed by an egg beater. Not unattractive. Something sleepily feline about her. I put her at twenty-five. Her grey rag seemed to have nothing under it but her.

"Mrs. Peterson home?" I asked pleasantly.

Her eyes narrowed. "You gonna buy the house?"

"I'll explain my business to Mrs. Peterson."

She faced the kid keeping his big eyes on her, muttered, "Damn sneakin' snoop!" Then nodded at me. "C'mon." And led me back to the mahogany door.

It was unlocked. I followed her swaying posterior across a nonfunctioning fountained patio, into one of those kitchens that could do everything but chew your food. All the formica, chrome, copper and whatnot glistened. You could have eaten off the tiled floor without a qualm.

She settled her softness into a white Breuer chair and nodded.

"I'm Alice Peterson. You buyin' the house?"

"Hunt, of Urban Indemnity," I said, smiling pleasantly at her.

"So what?"

Her placidity unravelled some of my pleasantness. I said, "We paid you nine hundred and ninety-five thousand over the past thirty months. For Johnson, Burns, Pryor, and Peterson.

"So what?"

"It's too coincidental."

"So what?"

A fascinating conversationalist. I didn't get to be Urban's Chief Investigator belaboring the obvious. I laid it on the line. "I'd like your permission to exhume Mr. Peterson and have him autopsied."

She thought about it. Her expression remained sullen, but I could tell she was thinking by the absent way her right hand nuzzled the bottom of her left breast. Softness nuzzling softness. It disturbed me.

So did the change creeping over her face. Mona Lisa appeared. That smile which isn't a smile... an almost sly curling of her lip. Glints peeked at me from her half-lidded eyes.

"Okay," she said.

I gaped at her, my brain racing. She was too sure of herself. She had what she considered a perfect murder method. An autopsy, she thought, could never discover it. She probably never heard of Doc Bernstein, whose ability to reconstruct a murder from a smear of blood or a drop of bile or a shred of tissue was legendary. I found my voice.

"Will you phone Sheriff White and tell him that?"

"It's disconnected." Indignation replaced Mona Lisa briefly. "I should give them fifteen dollars a month when I'll probably sell the house in a couple of weeks?"

A multi-millionaire miser. Mowing her own lawn, wearing a rag dress, skimping a lousy phone bill. I asked, "Will you tell him in person if I send Sheriff White down here?"

"Okay."

Gotcha! I thought. With that one word she had pricked the bubble of her multi-million dollar murder racket! My gaze became trapped by her moving fingers again, this time rubbing her right knee.

She had absently raised the skirt of her grey dress to do it. The knee was dimpled and golden tan. Under it her calf was full and tapering down nicely into what looked like army shoes. Golden tan into horsehide brown. I wondered if her toes were golden tan, if any part of her wasn't. If any part of her wasn't soft.

When my gaze finally returned to her Mona Lisa smile I caught a flicker of triumph in it.

And then it hit me. Like being caught from behind by a ten foot breaker. Seconds passed before I could recognize it through the hot and cold flashes leapfrogging through me. By then I was reeling.

Sex!

Not the slinky, teasy stuff Hollywood dishes out. Nothing to make you dream in terms of pastel boudoirs, frilly lingerie, exotic scents or whatever other superficial nonsense Hollywood, X-rated Cable or *Penthouse* photos have pinned on what makes the world go around.

What radiated from Alice Johnson, Burns, Pryor, Four, Five, Six, Seven, Eight, Peterson evoked visions of a bearskin rug in a dark corner of a warm cave.

Raw, unadulterated sex—right out of the primeval ooze.

It was there for me to see deep in her suddenly warm

brown eyes, in the squeeze-me golden tan of her bare arms, in her grey dress being pushed and pulled where it mattered most, in the moist ripeness of her parted lips. I had to fight down an urge to haul her off that chair and roll her under the kitchen table. I wanted to fondle her, squeeze her, kiss her, nibble on her. I wanted to crush that Mona Lisa smile in my mouth and chew on her full lips as if they were grapes.

I got out of there instead.

That big-eyed kid waiting near the abandoned mower backed away from my approach. I wasted a good five minutes trying to wheedle him into conversation, a "damn sneakin's-noop" being valuable in my line of work. But he wouldn't be wheedled. I filed him under "unfinished business", returned to my hotel and took a cold shower.

2

Sheriff White got her permission in person an hour later. Thirty minutes after that, we had a judicial order. It took two hours to exhume the late Mr. Peterson, and most of that night in the city morgue for Doc Bernstein to labor over his remains.

In the morning, Doc asked: "You want it in technical language, Bill?"

"No."

"Heart failure."

I did not belabor the point. Doc Bernstein was the best. I shipped him back to Manhattan on the next plane, then talked with Tom Willson, long distance.

"The hell you say!" he said when I gave him Doc's verdict.

I said, "She may have been lucky this time. We prepared to put big money into it?"

"How big?"

"For now, enough for eight more exhumations and autopsies?"

"Hell, yes!"

He switched the call to my assistant, Matt Norman, and I started the nationwide wheels turning. Then I left the hotel and prowled Tupelaca City, learning almost immediately that the Petersons had been wedded only six weeks.

"Out of this correspondence club," Barber Sam Vitelli, a crony of the late Roger Peterson I had gotten to by way of Sheriff White, told me.

He had been impressed by Alice's devotion to the deceased, always coming around to drag him home. "And economical?" In the mirror, I could see him shake his greyed head at the miracle of it. "She got rid of old Rog's servants—all four of 'em—and kept that big house cleaner all by herself than all four of 'em did together! And cook? What she could do with a mess o' catfish, man! You want me to cut more off the top?"

"No. That's fine. Why'd she want old Rog home all the time?"

In the mirror Barber Vitelli winked at me.

I spent the remainder of that day interviewing half a dozen other old gaffers referred by Sheriff White and Barber Vitalli, and returned to the hotel with their unanimous opinion that Alice Peterson had been a model wife, attentive to the needs of her December Groom every day of the six weeks of their marriage. They considered her frugal, but not miserly, as witness her sumptuous meals, of which all of them had frequently partaken, and what she had laid out for Old Rog's funeral, the most lavish Tupelaca City had ever seen.

Back at the hotel, I phoned New York and got men started on correspondence clubs. Matt Norman had news: "No trouble digging up Pryor, Bill."

"How'd he die?"

"Stroke. No sign of foul play. But there's a wrinkle. They cooperated in Cincinnati."

"Keep talking."

"She and Pryor signed a pre-marital agreement. It barred annulment, once they were hitched, for any cause."

"Figures. He might have tried to back out if he learned what happened to his predecessors."

"The lawyer who drew it up got a different impression. How she explained it, she'd been so taken by Pryor's letters, she didn't want the difference in their ages to make her change her mind before the stuff that got to her in his letters got to her in person. The lawyer said he believed her."

"He believed his hormones. Whose idea was this agreement?"

"Hers. She read to him from a list she had. The next clause pooled all assets into a common fund, which the lawyer thought real generous, since she came in with around half a million, while Pryor was worth only about half that."

"Those figures include insurance?"

"No."

"What else?"

"Both signatures would be necessary on any check or document withdrawing any of the aforementioned assets."

"Figures. Pryor may have turned spendthrift in his senility. Go ahead."

"In the event of a divorce—which, incidentally, could only be on the grounds of adultery—it would be 'no fault,' with each pulling out what he or she put in, with any increment split fifty-fifty, which the lawyer considered fair enough, although he didn't think Pryor had enough spare hormones to adulter much; while she—say, Bill, did you see her?"

"Yeah."

"According to people who knew her in Cincinnati, she sort of grew on you. She had something."

"She's still got it. That adultery clause was her escape hatch. In case her kill method misfired. She could ditch the guy and move on to the next. Anything else?"

"Survivor inherits all."

Naturally.

~

Next morning I went out and found Roger Peterson's executor, a gaffer entitled "Judge" Horace Cranshaw. He showed me a carbon of that pre-marital contract, identical to the one Matt Norman had described, and voiced the same meatheaded sentiments about it the Cincinnati lawyer had.

Back in the hotel, Matt Norman was on the line again.

"Dug up two more, Bill. Burns and one of Met's. Pneumonia and a massive heart attack. No sign of foul play in either. Each had signed that marriage contract and both had been snagged through a correspondence club. We nailed it. Bella Lovelorn's Romance Club. Alice met them through its bulletin, using the same ad every time. Can you beat it?"

"Leo Durocher didn't even change his socks when the New York Giants were on a winning streak."

"What's that, Bill?"

"My back teeth chattering. Anything else?"

"We traced her back to a town in Arkansas not far from Little Rock. Hames, Arkansas, née Dubronovich. Off a pig farm. Pigs and Dubronoviches have long since vanished, but we located an ex-boyfriend who can't forget Alice, even though he's been married four years."

"How far out of Little Rock?"

"About thirty minutes by bus. Fellow's name is Gilbert."

"Address?"

"Main Street. Runs the only feed store in town. Peter Gilbert."

~

It took me five hours, plane and bus, and ten minutes of fast talk before Peter Gilbert locked the front door, led me between sacks of grain and feed to a back room where he set an open jug of Mountain Dew on his desk between us.

"Can't forget her for a minute," he told me sorrowfully. He was sorrowful to look at, mostly eyeballs and teeth in a hollow-cheeked face. He seemed little more than a skeleton inside a blue work-shirt under faded overalls.

"That's fine!" I encouraged. "I want you to remember everything you can about her. Right down to the cradle."

"Ain't much point goin' that fur," he brooded. He inhaled some dew, offered me the jug. I passed. He sleeved his mouth. "Ain't much about Alice 'till she was eighteen. Before that, pigs. She grew up with 'em, slopped 'em. butchered 'em. Pigs."

"Start when she was eighteen, then," I suggested.

The Dew came around again. I passed again. He sighed.

"It was her smell."

I looked at him. Ke nodded solemnly.

"Hay ride. Up Jenkin's Road. I was beat outta takin' Jane —that's who I married—she got Alice. Figgered the whole ride for a bust. Pig girl. Won all the pie-bakin' contests at the Fairs, but never said much. Didn't look like much. Kinda sloppy, you know?"

I nodded.

Something flickered deep in his eyes. "Never forget it 'till the day I die. 'Bout ten minutes into that ride. Kind of chilly, an' we was hunkerin' down in the hay. I could hear Jane an' Bob Barbara—got kilt in Viet Nam—over the other side, him talkin' low an' her comin' out with sudden giggles. An' there I was with the pig girl. Feelin' nothin'. An' all of a sudden I smelled her. Alice. Not pigs. Not perfume. Somethin',—I dunno what. Mixed right in with the smell of hay an' all. It made me kinda reach over an' touch her.

He lapped some Dew without wasting further effort on fruitless hospitality. He went on: "Where I touched her it was kinda soft and warm. I sort of leaned over to where she lay lookin' up at me an' kissed her.

"I mean I bent down an' put my lips on hers, an' she jus' laid there doin' nothin' special, but it was like a couple a mean mules was kickin' me. I pulled up a little an' she asked me. 'Why'd you do that, Pete?' I told her, 'Alice, I gotta!', an' leaned over for more. Same thing. Like mules havin' at me. I got my hand under her dress an' felt where it was all soft an' warm an' hairy, kissin' her like crazy, an' when I pulled back for air, she asked, still cool, 'Why you doin' that, Pete?'

"Honest to God, I had no more effect on her than if she was back on the farm sloppin' pigs. 'Why'm I doin' it?' I gasps, feelin' hornier than a hound in heat. 'Aint you never been loved up before?'

"So help me, she jus' lay there, with me half on top of her an' the hay wagon kinda lurchin' from side to side an' us practically buried in the hay together like we was alone in the world, an' she says, 'No. Is this lovin'?"

"I jus 'went crazy. It was every part of me that touched any part of her caught on fire. I pushed down my pants and got all the way on top an' into her an' pantin', 'This is lovin', Darlin'! An' this... An' this..."

Gilbert broke off to reach for the jug. He had to wait his turn. The Dew went down my gullet like a stick of dynamite. When the smoke cleared, the jug was back on his desk and he was sleeving his mouth. He hitched his chair a bit closer.

"I tell you, Mr. Hunt, there was nothin' in this whole world like that hay ride. After awhile I jus' lay back breathin' hard, with Alice bendin' over me. 'Pete,' she says, 'how're you feelin'?' 'Wunnerful!' I kinda gasps. She asks me if that's what's meant by lovin'. I tell her that's it. She says it happens with pigs when they're in heat, on'y she figgered humans was different.

"We're so deep in the straw now, I can only see a couple a stars swingin' back an' forth. She grabs my hand and brings it inside her dress and all the way up 'till I'm grabbing her nipple, an' looks down at me real earnest-like. 'D'ya like how this feels, Pete?'

"Like it? Kee-rist! I had my second wind in nothin' flat! She reaches down and grabs my hard'n an' strokes it kinda, an' asks, 'You like me to do this, Pete? 'I damn near went crazy. I was all over her like a Texas tornado. I was on fire. I was runnin' hot an' cold all at once. An' right through that ride she kep' askin' me those damn questions. Like, 'You want me to kiss it, Pete? What should I do to make you like it more? You wanna kiss me there, Pete?' An' each time I'd gasp some kinda answer an' she'd do it an' it felt like my insides was full of firecrackers. An' in between I'd be layin' back an' wheezin' like an old locomotive huffin' up a steep grade, an'she'd come up with the next question.

"Her last was the best. It kicked the wind outta me. This was when we was almost back home in Hames, after she'd asked me if I'd ever loved up anyone else and I'd told her I'd gone to old Mamie's, on Pike Road, a couple of times. An' she'd asked me about that, an' I'd told her how Mamie's girls charged a buck for a short time, an' then I hadda explain that. An' that's when she popped that last question. Kinda mad like. She said, 'Well, Pete, ain't you gonna give me six bucks?'"

Gilbert's mournful glance deduced correctly that he wouldn't get the jug untilted from my face without mortal combat. He sighed and produced a fresh jug for himself.

I finally managed to choke out, "What then?"

"I gave her six bucks," he shrugged.

"I mean later. Between you and Alice?"

"Oh, it went on about a year," he said mournfully. "She was always willin'. All I hadda do was get near her an' I'd be ready to go. I didn't buy clothes or a car or nothin'. I kep' buyin' Alice. If I'd been workin' around the clock, without food or sleep, jus' let Alice be where I could smell her an' I'd be rarin' to go. One Sunday I hadda give her nine bucks!"

I allowed a reverent pause, then asked, "What finally broke it off?"

"Detective stories."

"Come again?"

"This feller who wrote 'em. I disremember his name. He stayed awhile at the Dubronovich farm. Fat feller. Lookin' for atmosphere, he said. Used to hang out with Doc Stanley an' Orrin Dullsworth. An' one night, after I'd taken Alice to the Fireman's Ball an' we'd drifted off to Harry Robert's back pasture later, an' I was all set to give her a tumble—wham!"

"Come again?"

Gilbert inhaled a seemingly endless swig of Mountain Dew. When the jug came down again his eyes were moist. He nodded solemnly.

"Her damn elbow right in my neck. She was madder'n hell. Said this detective story feller gave her five bucks every time. I told her, 'Honey, he's rich. All I got's the feed store.' An'then I got reckless. I mean smellin' her an' all. Pig girl or no. Sloppy or no. I told her, 'Alice, you can have everythin', I got, on'y I ain't got five dollars for every time. You marry me an' you can have everythin' I got, the feed store an' everythin'! She came up real close. I mean we was just sorta almost leanin' on each other an' the front of me was all on fire an' I was all set to! An'she whispered, 'I'll marry you, Pete, if you'll give me five bucks every time."

"I'll be damned!" I breathed.

"I was," Peter Gilbert nodded mournfully. "I asked her why for gosh sakes. An' she said she didn't like lovin'. The hottest piece o' love stuff I ever even hear about—an' she don't like lovin'! Even kissin'! She said it was like work. Like butcherin' pigs, or somethin'. I asked her why she'd let me love her up so damn much. She said she liked to find out about things. An' she was crazy about money. She was savin' as much as she could so she could run away from that damn pig farm. She wanted to go somewhere she could cook an' bake a lot. An' all this time we're belly to belly, me hotter'n hell. Finally I can't stand no more an' grab for her, an' this time it ain't no elbow in my neck. It's her fist. She like to near tore my head off. When I got up, she was gone. Jus' me alone in the pasture."

"Then what?"

"I went back to the dance an' drug Jane away from Bob Barbara an' drug her clear out to where I'd been talkin' to Alice, an' I tripped Jane right there. She tried to wriggle loose. She kep' clawin' an' punchin' an' I just closed my eyes an' thought of Alice an' kep' goin'. Pretty soon Jane was lickin' my jaw an' puttin' her tongue in my ear an' gaspin', 'I never knowed you felt this strong about me, Pete, darlin'!' We was still at it when the sun come up, an' folks saw us. So I hadda marry her."

"About Alice," I croaked. "What did she do?"

"Her paw was in town a couple days later. Said she'd dug up all his savin's an' vamoosed. 'Bout a year later the whole kit an' caboodle o' Dubronoviches hauled up an' cleared out. An' good riddance!"

Gilbert brooded awhile, then shook his head sorrowfully. "Cain't ever get Alice outta my mind. Jane thinks it's her. Brags what a hot lovin' man she's got. Every time I crawl into bed with Jane I close my eyes an' think of Alice an'—wham!"

"Wham!" I echoed solemnly, getting to my feet. The floor

tried to get up with me. I hung on to his desk until it settled. Gilbert remained hunched over his jug, brooding. I asked, "On Pike Road?"

He nodded. "Grey house. Over the hill, just past the post office. Tell Mamie I sent you."

~

I told Mamie nothing. The fresh air restored enough of my perspective to send me U-turning back into Gilbert's feed store. He was still hunched over the jug. I said, "Okay. You can't remember this detective story writer's name. But you mentioned a Doc Stanley and someone named Orrin Dullsworth. That a real doctor? And what does Dullsworth do?"

It turned out to be Doctor Jackson Stanley. And Dullsworth was an attorney, son of Judge Dullsworth, in Little Rock. And both gentlemen had abandoned Hames about a year after Alice's sudden departure.

Back in my Tupelaca City hotel room about five hours later, after what I thought had been a business-like conversation, Matt Norman, asked:

"Bill, are you tight?"

"Was."

"You still sound fuzzy. Did you hear what I told you?"

"Sure. We've now autopsied all nine stiffs, with nary a sign of skullduggery. You got Bella Lovelorn cooperating. Alice sent her tenth ad yesterday. And Bella, who seems to be a guy named Schultz, agrees to hold back all replies until we give her, him, whatever, the office. Right?"

His sigh traveled a thousand miles into my waiting ear. "Bill, you're still tight."

"Right!"

I broke the connection and went to bed.

3

Next morning I drove my rented Chevy out to where I had a field glass view of the shell-lined driveway. In my pocket lay a dictated copy of her Bella Lovelorn ad:

PRETTY YOUNG WIDOW.

>*Rich men go crazy for me, but I can't stand kids. No kids apply. I want to meet a nice widower in his sixties who appreciates good cooking. I'm a prize-winning cook and real affectionate. And I am lonesome for a good loving man who appreciates good eating and good loving.*
>
>*Brown Eyes*

Shakespeare may have laughed himself sick, but did Shakespeare ever net almost ten million American dollars with that little writing?

I sat in the car and watched the same big-eyed kid I had seen the first day. He seemed to make a career of hanging around. Twice Alice's face and fist appeared in windows; her face scowling, her fist shaking. The kid just stood there. A scrawny tyke, about twelve. He yelled something at her, but my field glasses failed to bring me his words.

The third time, she emerged to chase him. A replica of my first visit, a zigzag chase across the lawn. I realized now that it wasn't that Alice was slow or clumsy; just that the kid's footwork was magnificent. He never ran two steps if one would do. In the end it was like the other time. Alice heaved shells from the driveway's border and the kid kept sidestepping them. Her aim was still lousy.

She finally disappeared behind the mahogany door and the kid walked toward me. When he got close enough I saw he'd been crying. As he passed, I called, "Hey, Buster—"

He shot me a frightened glance and started running.

I did not get to be Urban's chief investigator fattening my bottom. His footwork was fancy, but I was able to match him, zig for zag. At that, we must have been almost half a mile away from the car before I caught a handful of his Miami Dolphins T-shirt.

Then my life became full of him. He was geared for confusion. He kicked my shin. Twice. He bit my wrist. He punched my—well, it was a low blow.

I finally got him down. I spread over him like a blanket. He was sobbing as if his heart would break, saying, "If she'd on'y tell me how she does it! I'd be able to knock you out right now!"

"Come again?" I winced down into his tear-streaked face.

"How's she do it?" he wailed to the cloud-dappled sky somewhere over the back of my head. "When Mr. Peterson rassled her he'd get her down, jus' like you got me. An' then she'd do somethin'. I couldn't see what, but it was like he was knocked out. He jus' rolled off'n her an' lay there like he was asleep. I keep askin' an' beggin' her t'tell me, but all she does is chase me an' call me names. If she'd teach me that trick, I'd whup that damn Calvin who's allus pickin' on me in school!"

"Rasslin'?" choked out of me.

"I usta think Mr. Peterson was winnin'. Because he'd be on top. But she'd allus pull that trick, an' he'd jus' roll off'n her like he was dead."

I talked him into a secluded booth in a sweetery entitled The Gum Drop, where I gulped black coffee and watched his tremendous eyes over a straw buried in a chocolate malted. His name, appropriately, was Tommy.

He said the first time he saw the Petersons "wrestle" was when he took a shortcut across their lawn one Sunday morning on his way to a fishing hole and "happened" to peek in their kitchen window. Alice, he noted, instead of sitting across from Roger at the breakfast table, was up and performing some kind of dance.

"What kind?" I cut in.

He abandoned the straw momentarily. "Wiggle dance. It made me feel all funny inside. Old Mr. Peterson was lookin' at her an' laughin', an' his face was all red-like. An'she kicked off a shoe an' it went sailin' right by his head. An' then she kicked off the other. An' then she kinda wiggled outta her dress an' Mr. Peterson jumped up an' grabbed her.

"I never seen anybody like to rassle like old Mr. Peterson. I thought he was winnin'. He had her on the floor an' she kep' tryin' to shake him off—an' then it happened."

"She pulled that trick, huh?"

His eyes flooded. "If she'd on'y tell me! All of a sudden it was like he fell asleep, or somethin'. An 'she jus' rolled him off. Then she got up an' put on her dress. Then she picked him up like he was a baby an' carried him into the bedroom."

"Just like that!" I breathed.

"So I went aroun' t' the bedroom windows," Peeping Tommy went on, "an' I'm never so surprised in my whole life. Mr. Peterson's woke up again an' he was rasslin' her all over the bed!"

Poor Peterson! Poor Peterson? What a way to shuffle off this mortal coil!

"An' the same thing happens—"

"I know, Tommy. I know. Old Peterson's winning—because he's on top. Then—blooie!—and he's a sack of bones! I know. And maybe an hour later they probably gave the mattress another beating."

"Not the bed." Tommy's straw sucked air. I signaled for a refill. He said, "On the rug in the living room. And it was that night, when I was comin' home from fishin'. It looked so crazy. She don't like to wear no clothes, Missus Peterson, you know that?"

My eyebrows wigwagged him on.

"She was layin' on the floor real still an' all over her was raisins. I mean scattered all over her like. An' Mr. Peterson was crawlin' around an' lickin' 'em up with his tongue, an'—"

She "won" again.

Twenty-five to his sixty-eight, not to mention she probably grew stronger as they went along, not deriving orgasms from it, merely exercise. While he? He naturally grew weaker and weaker. Until: "natural causes."

I was reeling. There never was a murder method like this before. Legal all the way down the line. And her pre-marital contract made it foolproof. The gaffers could not resist her squeeze-me softness, her kiss-me lips, the waves radiating from her Mona Lisa smile, not to overlook the little erotic wrinkles she had picked up along the way to tease them into super-human effort. Raw, basic sex. On the floor, in bed, probably in the bathtub. Every hour on the hour—running out to drag them home days—probably waking them during the nights. And if the guy didn't cave in, there was always the adultery clause in that pre-marital contract. She'd simply adulter a bit, get "caught," get divorced, pick up her marbles and go hunt her next victim.

Cold-blooded, hot-blooded murder. The intent cold, the method hot.

I left Peeping Tommy on his third malted, with a day's unlimited credit from The Gum Drop. I walked back to my rented flivver and drove it up the shell-lined driveway to the mahogany door. After checking my hair comb, adjusting my tie and pasting a warm smile on my face, I used the brass knocker.

4

She wore green. The same sullen eyes, pouting lips, wind-swept hair. But no army shoes. No shoes. She was golden tan right down to the floor.

"Now what?"

"Let's talk."

"I got nothin' to talk to you about."

"Let's talk about Johnson, Burns, Pryor, Four, Five, Six, Seven, Eight and Peterson—and how you murdered them."

She smiled. No longer sullen or pouting. Mona Lisa was back. Peter Gilbert had been right. I could smell her. Not perfume. Certainly not pigs. Alice. Alice was enough. I did not want to stand there. It was growing dark and slightly chilly. I wanted in. I said, "Alice, won't you be wanting more insurance checks in the years to come?"

"You're just a detective."

"Chief of Investigations," I corrected her softly.

Interest glittered deep in her lidded eyes. They checked the shine in my shoes, the crease in my trousers, the slenderness of my hips, the bulge of my chest, my chin, my mouth, my nose. When she was back to my hot, anxious stare, she said, as softly, "You think you found out somethin'?"

"Everything."

She said, "Honey, let's go inside."

Her undulations wigwagged me across the patio and into what turned out to be her living room where she settled the best of them in the soft upholstery of a green divan. She didn't seem to mind me settling alongside her. It gave her my left knee on which to rest a golden tan hand. She asked, "Whaddya think you found out, honey?"

"You killed them with love. Morning, noon, and night. You loved them to death. Literally."

Her face darkened. "That damn snoopin' kid!"

I patted her hand on my knee. Like patting a charge of tiny sparks. I left my hand there.

"He's just a kid. He thinks you were wrestling. What you have to worry about is all the insurance companies ganging up on you."

Her grip on my knee intensified. "Why, honey? When folks get married ain't they supposed t'love each other up?"

"Sure, but insurance companies take a dim view of losing all those premiums they'd have collected had those nine guys lived out their allotted three score and ten, and possibly longer."

"Ain't it their hard luck?"

"I guess it was our old friend of the detective stories who gave you the idea in the first place."

"You know Peter Paige?"

"And Orrin Dullsworth probably drew up your premarital contract, with Old Doc Jack Stanley teaching you what in a gaffer would qualify him for your specialty—"

Her hand shook my knee. "Never mind them. What can the insurance companies do?"

My free hand had sort of wandered up behind the divan to rest on her soft shoulder where it began smoldering. I was getting a bit giddy from the musky smell of her.

"All sorts of things," I murmured, thinking that was why ancient peoples had Goddesses instead of Gods. Women like this. Earth Mothers, from whom all good things flowed, and to whom it all flowed back in time. What radiated from her was probably even older than Gods and Goddesses, back to the beginnings of Time, when the first he-jellyfish responded to the first she-jellyfish wriggling by. "All sorts of things," I repeated, and closed the space between our lips.

She didn't move, didn't flicker an eyelash, but it was as if my spine rolled up tight, then snapped out again, as if my ears popped, as if smoke steamed out of my eyes, as if my breath was cut off—but that was her elbow.

"How?" she insisted.

"Baby—" I said.

"You agreed lovin's legal!" she said.

"Sure," I said. "But you're bucking some of the richest companies in the world." I leaned toward her, but her elbow started up again.

"What can they do?" she demanded.

"Baby," I pleaded.

"Well, can they do somethin'?"

"Baby, you're a living, breathing aphrodisiac!"

"What's that?"

"What puts a charge of love in a man's shoes and blows his hat off."

"You talk real pretty," she whispered, leaning back toward me. Then closed the gap. Her tongue became alive against mine. My arms melted around her and we grew tighter than two snakes in a garden hose, but it wasn't enough. Not nearly tight enough. I would have to spend years of practicing to get tight enough.

My mind danced to Peter Gilbert's tale of the glorious bucks. And then my mind winced. What was the ante now?

My thoughts charged forward again. On my fifty-five thousand a year, with my IRAs and CDs, and my own hundred and fifty grand twenty-payment life policy, and all those little investigatory wrinkles I'd figured out through the years but never scrupled to hazard...

Suppose I did wind up like One-to-Peterson? It would take so much longer. Still in my prime. Meat on my bones. Eyes clear. Heart strong. Worked out and jogged regularly. It would take maybe decades longer. And then well—what a way to die!

That thing cutting off my wind was not passion. Her elbow again.

"Say, now!"

"Baby—"

"You ain't answered me. How can the insurance companies gang up?"

I got up and limped a brief tour of the green broadloom, imagining her supine on it and Old Peterson crawling over her, nibbling raisins. God! I sat beside her again. One golden tan mound was almost out of her green dress. And most of her golden tan thighs. All of her was golden tan, except the glitter in her unsmiling brown eyes.

"Well?"

"All sorts of ways." I gestured vaguely. "They could stick to you close as a corn plaster. Keep you from ever wedding Number Ten. Warn each prospect off as soon as you found him. We're powerful enough to bend a law here and there. We'd invest tens of thousands to keep you from hooking us for hundreds of thousands—"

"That ain't legal!" she burst out indignantly.

I did not laugh. Her waves were too compelling. "Baby—" I murmured, reaching for her again. Her elbow stayed down. In her eyes seeped that ageless 'come and get it, you fool!' expression.

"You said 'we.'" she breathed, practically into my lips.

"Me, baby," I barely breathed. Her lips brushed lightly across mine.

"You mean nobody else at all?"

"Me. Bill Hunt. I make fifty-five grand a year. I'm insured for a hundred and fifty. Almost that much invested. And ways to euchre Urban that would put yours to shame! The two of us, baby—"

What she was allowing my hands to do dried my throat.

"But why should all those other companies leave it up to you?"

"Urban's hit hardest. The others put it in our lap. Meaning our Bureau of Investigation. Meaning me. Me—"

"I can marry again, darlin'?" she murmured.

"Me, baby. We'll—" The tip of her tongue touring my lips froze me motionless.

"An' you'll always be there?"

"Always! Beside you, behind you, under you—any way you—"

"Suppose they fire you an' send someone else?" she breathed.

"We'll bamboozle 'em! We'll catch that peeping midget and bury him in the foundation of our love nest. We'll—"

"You ain't makin' sense!"

"What I've got to make, Baby, is you."

"An' you're the only one? It's all up to you?"

"Was, Baby. I've been outranked. From here in, it will be up to you! Starting right now!"

"Now!" she echoed through a widening smile that suspended my breathing. She gently returned me my hands. I watched, as if paralyzed, as her fingers entered the cleft between her golden tan globes and tightened around the green fabric. The ripping of it all the way down the front of her was like the crescendoing chords of a symphony orchestra in my surging bloodstream.

And there she was. Willowy curves right down to the green broadloom. Soft gold tan everywhere except for a thin V of whiter skin embracing the widest part of her hips and dipping to her crotch. I could feel the bearskin rug, the warm corner of the dark cave. My ears roared. I barely noticed her fingers swiftly unbuttoning my shirt, releasing my belt, unzipping my fly.

This time her lips and tongue were alive against mine while her busy fingers kept at it—to leave nothing between us but us. And it almost became like that... tingling sparks stitching all of her to all of me; hot, tingling sparks from the warmth of her flesh—and something cold.

Cold?

Icy!

Reflex jerked my arm down. Thought had nothing to do with it. My idiot thoughts were still wallowing in the warm corner of a dark cave. But years of conditioning had trained automatic responses. Reflex yanked my wrist down, deflecting the icy touch enough for its blast to do no more than sting my bare side.

She was scrambling to her feet behind the silver revolver she had snagged—probably from behind one of the divan's cushions. She was screaming at me, every inch of her quivering with hitherto suppressed rage.

She had every right to shoot dead a widow-raping son of a bitch like me, didn't she? I'd ripped off her dress and attacked her, hadn't I? Hound her, would I? Suck around her for the rest of her life, was that my stupid idea? If all that stood between success and failure of her next marriage was widow-raping son of a bitch me, why, she would straighten that out right now!

All of which I heard in transit.

Her second shot tore into the green broadloom inches from where I was tumbling over it. Her third caught a lamp-shade alongside the window. Her fourth entered the window where its screen used to be.

The screen was preceding me out of the living room. The flagstoned patio fed me a chin-to-toe uppercut, then sprouted flying chips inches from my left ear. That was number five.

Number Six lost itself against the inside of the patio wall as I scrambled a zigzag route toward the mahogany door. That was the clip. I stopped and looked back. Her golden tan body was framed in window glow as she pointed the revolver at me with both hands and garnered a futile click.

I buttoned my shirt, zippered my trousers, checked for the wallet in my hip pocket. Then, leaving my jacket back there in her living room, I went out the mahogany door, got into the rented heap and drove back to the hotel.

5

"Why me? Why not Matt?" Tom Willson objected, when they finally tracked him to his Scarsdale home long distance.

"Because Matt can't make the sort of decisions you can," I told him. I could hear voices and laughter behind him, as if my call had brought him away from a party.

"What sort of decisions?"

"Whether you want to go on with it. It might mean tracking down a detective story writer, Peter Paige; a doctor, Jack Stanley; and a lawyer, Orrin Dullsworth. But even if we laid out the kind of dough that would entail, and it was established they'd cooked up and masterminded the deal, and even shared in the loot, I don't see what we could do about it. And even if we did, the amount saved would actually be a certain quantity of premium money that might not add up to the expenditures. See what I mean?"

"That's as clear as mud!" he expostulated.

"Okay," I said. "Try this for size. She loved them to death."

"Once more?"

"She's got one talent: sex. Flaming hot. You'd have to get in range to believe it. One trick—using it to weaken the resistance of gaffers until whatever ails them takes over. And she has one passion: money. No way we could bribe her to stop. We couldn't begin to offer her what she nets for herself doing what comes naturally. And they'd laugh us out of any court in the land if we try getting her convicted of sexing nine old men to death. As she put it to me: 'Ain't a wife an' husband supposed to love each other up?'"

"I'll be damned!" Him, me, Peter Gilbert—but at least

45

Gilbert got nine glorious reprieves from damnation one glorious Sunday!

"For what it's worth," I said wearily, "right now all I can think is wash our hands of it. Just let her go on until she wears out."

"How do you figure that?"

"It's the cost factor. What we actually lose in estimated premium money versus the expense of keeping men on her from here on in—to warn off prospective Number Tens. Which maybe wouldn't work anyhow if any of them got in range of her. She's something that's got to be experienced to be believed. Not to overlook that many of the prospects would have paid up life policies, in which case it would only be the interest on their premiums we'd be getting. See what I mean?"

Instead of a reply, I was treated to several minutes of background voices and laughter before Tom Willson's voice returned to my ear.

"Bill?"

"Yeah?"

"That's out of the question. We can't let her keep on getting away with it. You're going to have to find a way to stop her."

"For crying out loud, ask me to stop the sun, the tides, the change of seasons, the grass from growing! How the hell can she be stopped?"

"Urban pays you a damn good salary to figure answers to a question like that. You hear me, Bill? Stop her!"

I had an answer for that. But he killed the connection before I could utter it.

~

I sat in a northbound plane and put it into writing. My

resignation. Short of having Alice killed, how could she be stopped?

Take her to court? The judge would get one whiff of her and he would tot up his savings, check on his insurance, and be knocking on her door the first thing next morning, begging to become Number Ten, as I almost had, knowing he would wind up nothing but eyeballs and teeth, like Peter Gilbert, and drooling at the prospect.

Hound her? She could sue, and that same judge would probably give her Urban Indemnity, lock, stock and barrel. Even her nine victims, could they be resurrected, would probably agree it had been worth it; every dipsy-doodle second of it!

But not to Urban. To Urban she was a living murder weapon. Absolutely foolproof. No law could punish, or even stop her. They had invented ack-ack as a defense against bombers, bazookas against tanks, depth charges against submarines, armored vests against pistol bullets. For every weapon a defense had been devised—one probably in the works right now against nuclear fission or fusion. But what defense was possible against irresistible sex?

The stewardess was bending over me anxiously. "You're looking pale, sir, are you all right?"

"Fine," I lied.

She was pretty, but no Earth Goddess. I leaned back and closed my eyes and wondered how Oscar Carlson would advise me. Ever since my dad passed away when I was five, I had taken my problems to Oscar and he usually came through. And thinking of what he might say–it was almost as if I heard him say it. Incredibly, in that brief flash of insight I had the answer to Alice Johnson, Pryor, Burns, Four, Five, Six, Seven, Eight, Peterson; the perfect defense against homicidal sex!

6

I destroyed my resignation in the cab en route to the Queens construction job where I knew I would find Oscar.

He was sitting behind his pipe in the watchman's shack; big, gray-haired, China-blue eyes in a pink face. He removed the pipe and grinned his fine white teeth at me. "Billy! What a nice surprise!" He limped toward me, still hindered by the shrapnel wound he had gotten crawling through alien mud to drag my wounded dad back from no-man's land.

We pumped hands. We slapped shoulders. He had refused all my efforts to aid him through the years. The wound had left him fit only for a meager pension and jobs such as this. But he had kept saying, "You take care of yourself, Billy. I'll take care of Oscar. Come see me once in a while. That's all."

I grinned up into his kindly face. "Oscar, suppose you had a couple of million bucks?"

He took it calmly, puffing judiciously on his pipe. Most of my youth I had asked him sillier-sounding questions. He finally removed the pipe and said, "Hotel or dairy farm. My folks was hotel people back in the old country. And when I was a boy, while they were having a hard time getting the hotel going, they sent me to an uncle's who had a big dairy farm. Holsteins. I had a feel for that, but when I came here—"

He did not have to elaborate. The draft practically snagged him right off the boat. And after the war he had nothing to look forward to but the pension and watchman-type jobs. I grinned up at him.

"Where'd they be, Oscar?"

"Upstate," he said wistfully. "That's good dairy country. Lots of clover and alfalfa."

"We'll get you the best," I assured him.

His eyes twinkled. "You gonna buy me a farm, Billy?"

"And a hotel, or motel. Whichever is handiest," I said. "Urban will set it up. But you'll do the buying out of the almost ten million you're going to marry."

And then I told him all about Alice. Just as I've told it here. From her endorsements on nine insurance checks to her simple-minded assumption that killing me would deter the insurance companies from hindering her future operations. Long before I was done, Oscar was laughing. By the end, tears streamed down his cheeks. "What a gal!" he gasped. "And you were willin' to die, Billy?"

"But not you," I told him softly. "Not somebody with the willpower of Oscar Carlson. Not for almost ten million dollars worth of hotel and dairy farm—hey, Oscar?"

He sucked fiercely on his pipe, filling that small shack with cloud. Then he shook his greyed head regretfully. "Nah, Billy. It'd be nice but it's too dirty."

"Dirty!" I was outraged. "After she murdered nine innocent men? Not to mention stealing all that loot! They give ten years to hungry kids holding up groceries. Where do you get off, dirty?"

He frowned. "Wal, if you put it like that—"

I put it like that. I put it other ways. I put it to him like a crack insurance agent working on a sweepstakes winner. In the end he was raising half-hearted objections, like how could he interest Alice with only his pension, eighty bucks in a savings account and only his G.I. insurance.

And I knew I had him.

7

Five days later the following nestled in Alice's box in Bella Lovelorn's Romance Club:

Dear Brown Eyes,

I read your sweet letter in the bulletin and thought right away this girl is no gold digger. My old friend, Banker Maurer, is always telling me, "Oscar, you can't take all that money with you. Get married and have children. Marry someone young enough to give you children." I'd tell him I was scared of falling for a gold digger. But you don't seem like one. Your letter made me realize this thousand acre dairy farm is so lonesome. And who will run my fifty unit motel if I die? Won't you answer, dear Brown Eyes?

Hoping,
Oscar Carlson

Her reply was prompt, airmail and special delivery:

Darling Oscar,

I know I shouldn't call you darling so soon, but your letter was so beautiful. I felt I knew you well enough to call you darling. Darling! I'm no gold digger. My late husband left me well fixed. But I am lonesome, darling. I need to be loved by someone like you, Oscar, darling. Kids just bore me. I need an older man who's not afraid to give me all the good loving I need.

How old are you, and how is your health, my sweet darling?

Love,
Alice Peterson
(Brown Eyes)

Obviously, she cooked up her own masterpieces. I had a psychologist and two professional love story writers cook up Oscar's reply:

Dearest Alice Brown Eyes,

Your letter thrilled me so much, I couldn't sleep. I am sixty-five years old, but don't let that fool you. I can love better than a much younger man, even though I had that heart attack three years ago. I have been thinking my three hundred thousand dollar insurance policy is not enough. It goes to charity now. But my wife and children would need much more. Should I fly down there? Or should I send my plane to fly you here? You can stay at my motel, The Carlson, while you are here.

Please answer me soon, my darling Brown Eyes.
I Love You Already,
Your Oscar

She answered in person.

My ops told me how her eyes glistened at the brand new THE CARLSON on the huge slowly rotating sign on the busy four-lane highway. She almost drooled over the rolling pastures and neat barns and silo on the thousand-acre dairy farm behind the motel.

Banker Maurer, who knew on which side his mortgages were buttered, titilated her by fawning over Oscar as if he was a Rockefeller in disguise. As a matter of fact, he contributed in the little drama enacted for her behalf in the lawyer's office when Oscar, reading the pre-nuptial agreement, got angry over the divorce-for-adultery clause. "No adultery!" Oscar shouted, then sank back in a chair clutching his chest. Banker Maurer pleaded: "Oscar, remember what the doctor told you about getting excited!" And while Oscar slumped there, gasping for air, the lawyer asked Alice, "Can't we change that a little? Say, in the event of adultery, the injured party would get the entire estate?"

Alice, who couldn't take her eyes off Oscar slumped in the chair and gasping, said, "Sure, whatever dear Oscar wants—"

And so it was done in quadruplicate, the fourth copy landing in Maurer's vault.

Later, Oscar told me of their wedding night, a honeymoon at home. Why, she had urged, waste a lot of money at some other motel or hotel when they'd want to be private most of the time anyhow?

She fashioned a supper that had Oscar's juices gurgling in ecstasy. Following which, she sat him before the huge television screen with an open bottle of brandy and a glass at his elbow, while she went back to the kitchen to do the dishes.

Oscar enjoyed the television, as he always did, never minding or caring what program was on, relishing the commercials as well. And eventually he grew aware she had returned from the kitchen and was sitting at his feet, leaving him a bird's eye view of what the low-cut V of her diaphanous gown barely covered. She was just sitting there, letting her old black magic percolate.

And after awhile, she laid a hand on his thigh, exposed him to her million volt eye-power and softly suggested, "I'm just dyin' to love you up, Darlin'. Think you could carry me to bed?"

Oscar sighed, having dreaded this moment. "Maybe we better get a couple things straight first," he said compassionately. "I know all about the nine fellers you killed. Billy Hunt fixed up this marriage to stop you."

He told me she just froze there at his feet. She whispered, "But you're rich, ain't you, Darlin'?"

"I ain't got a dime," he said sadly.

"But this farm!"

"Urban gave me a mortgage on it, countin' on your money."

She squeaked, "The insurance?"

"I got a policy, yah," Oscar nodded unhappily. "Only I ain't able to pay the premiums. Urban figured you would."

"The motel?"

"Same thing. Urban figured you'd pick up the mortgage."

She came off the floor behind poised nails, trying for his

eyes and wound up across his knees, getting his disciplinary palm, Oscar never having been one for nonsense.

She screamed she'd get an annulment for fraud. He gently reminded her, between whacks, their contract prohibited annulments for any reason whatsover. She screamed about divorce. Patiently, he reminded her that only adultery was allowed by the contract, in which event the injured party would inherit all. Her only realistic option was to accept the inevitable and settle down to a life of dairy farming and motel management.

Came her tears. Oscar, being a gentle-hearted soul, soothed her in his arms. Pretty soon the soothing became mutual, with cunning little touches contributed by Alice. Like nibbling his ear lobe. Running her tongue along the underside of his jaw. Applying her lips to his and introducing him to her agile tongue.

In the process, her fingers expertly began disengaging him from such encumbrances as his shirt, his trousers, his under-things. Her almost transparent robe seemed to melt away of its own accord.

If she couldn't get him out of her life one way, didn't the contract still stipulate that survivor inherited all?

But she reckoned without the iron willpower of Oscar Carlson.

Ten minutes later she stood before him in her superb alto-gether, screaming words at him he never knew had been coined, which brought her bare amplitude back for another stern session with his big palm.

Following which, she dressed, packed a suitcase and fled.

8

A month later, one of my ops interrupted a wedding in Oregon with words that sent Alice running to the street, leaving behind a bewildered Justice of the Peace and a flabber-gasted gaffer, aged sixty-three.

Two months later, in a small church in Arizona, ditto.

She forsook bigamy, but with only one marketable talent, the going was rough. Every time she tried to cash a check for her own money she was politely informed her husband's signature was also required on it. What remained was that single talent. But having tasted hundred thousand dollar scores, the tens and twenties she garnered to enable her to keep eating were as wormwood to her miserly soul.

Still, it was almost a full year before she reappeared at the farm, told Oscar, "I got a right to be here," made her way to a bedroom and began unpacking.

I followed her in at the head of a small army, including the local sheriff, some of his men and some of mine. While two of his men held her, completed the unpacking. When I was done, the bureau top held a vial of cyanide, a can of rat poison, a saw-toothed hunting knife and a loaded .32 caliber Smith & Wesson revolver.

The sheriff, who knew where his next campaign funds were coming from, looked at me. I looked at Oscar standing unhappily in the doorway.

"We can put her away," I told him, actually telling her. "She'll get five to ten for violating the Sullivan Law alone."

He shook his head. "Don't jail her, Billy. She'll come to her senses."

I told her dull, expressionless face, "Killing Oscar would have gotten you zilch. You've never been out of our sight for a minute. Even had you done it, it wouldn't net you a red cent. In this state you can't profit from a felony."

"I wanna go," she said dully.

"In a minute," I grinned at her. I motioned Matt Norman for the folio. From it I took fifteen blow-ups, laid them side by side on the bed and went from one to the other like a museum guide:

"This one's Alice and a bartender in Denver named Malone. That one's Alice and Craig, a Fresno car salesman. Here she is with a Los Angeles cop, Mendoza—"

I called them off, one by one; Alice and her whilom clientele. Three in positions I had never seen before. All taken on infrared film. Most of them caught her face, some from the damnedest angles.

I looked up from the last to Oscar's troubled countenance. "Pick up the marbles, Pal. Adultery. You've got her on it fifteen times."

He seemed on the verge of tears. "I didn't want it like this, Billy. I thought she'd come home an' settle down when she found what a good thing I'm makin' of the farm an' motel. Another eight years an' they'll have paid for themselves."

Alice stirred. She had been standing like a vertical corpse. Now her hips shifted slightly and that room became charged. Matt Norman, who had been gathering the blow-ups to return them to the folio, turned like a bird dog catching a sudden scent. The sheriff appeared to have trouble breathing. I caught myself thinking, with my fifty-five thousand a year—

Right out of the primeval ooze. All it took was a flick of her hips to turn it on. That room throbbed.

"Eight years?" she breathed.

Oscar nodded.

"You mean in eight years we'd have all the money back, and the farm and the motel?"

"Wouldn't surprise me one little bit," I grinned. "She loves money, and he's making it. He loves her cooking."

The sheriff muttered, "Even so—"

"My dad was his sergeant," I told him. "My dad, an old style nightstick cop from Hell's Kitchen, was probably one of the nastiest sergeants in the U.S. Infantry. He made Oscar's life a living hell. Oscar just took it with a gentle smile, and that made my dad pick on him more. But when my dad lay wounded in no-man's land, it was Oscar who crawled out in broad daylight and brought him in, netting a hunk of shrapnel in the process. My dad was a reformed man for the rest of his life, and Oscar was his best friend. You might say he's a born reformer, a do as he does, not a do as he says, kind of guy."

A couple of cigarettes later, Oscar and Alice appeared in the doorway, hand in hand. Her face glowed like a bride's. He was scarlet, but grinning. "No more trouble, Billy. Alice will stay home from now on.

Then he handed me the double-signature check that paid off the two mortgages, brought the premiums on his three hundred grand policy up to date and jumped me to the next income tax bracket at Urban.

That was enough years ago for the flourishing farm and motel to have paid for themselves at least one and a half times over. No longer an Earth Goddess, Alice Carlson's solitary passions remain money—and cooking. Oscar, to her, has become the personification of money. Her idea of a happy evening is to sit at his feet and hear him talk overhead, milk prices, and profits, especially profits. Mona Lisa lies buried under layers of contented fat, which, nowadays, is shared by Oscar, all the fat a tribute to her sensational cookery.

And so you might say they lived happily ever after.

Although Oscar refuses to let me erect a small monument on the lawn of their farmhouse in tribute to the device that enabled him, and Urban, to once and for all put an end to the homicidal progress of Alice Johnson, Pryor, Burns, Four, Five, Six, Seven, Eight, Peterson—and now Carlson.

The hunk of shrapnel he acquired dragging my dad out of no-man's land.

It castrated him.

to be, or be to not

I HAD BARELY OCCUPIED my usual luncheon table at The Gourmand when I noticed the large man appear in the doorway. He surveyed the scattering of diners, then headed directly to my table. Occupying the chair across from mine and regarding me with an expression curiously compounded of triumph and pity, he said, "That's the first copy sold in Manhattan the past eleven months." His square chin indicated my recent purchase lying face down beside my fork. "I reached the bookshop as you walked out with it. Lost track of you awhile. You're such an inconspicuous little fellow. But then I spotted you coming in here."

He seemed unlike the sort to be interested in Lee Chin's *Lotus Leaves*, looking more like a down-to-earth businessman. Probably in his mid-forties, his portly frame was garbed conservatively in charcoal grey. The China blue of his eyes set off his ruddy complexion and greying brown hair.

"I doubt if there's a philosophical type," he said dryly, as if my thought had been voiced. "Matter of fact, the man I'm after is no recognizable type. Even the way he knocked off the Donnerville National was characteristically uncharacteristic."

He allowed a pause to acquire significance.

"A bank robber?" I managed to murmur.

He shrugged. "Even that might be considered moot. Although he did walk out with almost a million. Last year. You probably read about it."

"I'm afraid not," I lied. "Crime news depresses me. Are you a police officer?"

"Detective Lieutenant. Name's Carmichael."

"Smith," I said.

His tone was polite. "John?"

"Peter Smith," I said. "Are you implying a relationship between this moot criminal and my purchase of Lee Chin's *Lotus Leaves*?"

"Or had you purchased Buddha's *Tripitika*, or the *Upanishads*, or *The Zend Avesta*, or Confucius' *Analects*. Last indication was that Harvey Matson was on an Oriental philosophy kick, although that's not necessarily indicative. Before that, he —" His voice trailed off. "Am I boring you, Mister—ah—Smith?"

He fascinated me. I asked, "Will you join me for lunch? The cuisine here is simple and American, but superb."

"I like that 'but'," he said. "Whatever you're having. But it must be on my expense account. There a waiter handy?"

"At your elbow," I smiled, for his gaze had clung to me unwaveringly.

Now he glanced briefly at Tony and said, "Whatever this gentleman is having," and, when Tony retired with our double order, told me, "My problem seems to turn on a point of philosophy, one, in fact, Lee Chin was driving at in a *Lotus Leaves* parable."

I said, "I'm somewhat of a philosophical amateur."

"By definition, practically everyone is," he shrugged. "But you'd have an opinion, say, on Leibniz?"

"Only that I doubt his monads could be entirely window-less," I said, causing his eyes to glisten.

"Exactly Harvey Matson's point in one of his flyleaf scribbles I found. But that was a good month after the heist, two weeks after I'd been assigned, and the trail was cold both ways, into his past and up to here. His philosophical bent was the most significant identifying characteristic emerging from two weeks of interviews in Donnerville, even including one with his wife, Penelope, barely an hour before she vanished."

"To join him in hiding?" I asked.

"I doubt it," he shrugged. "More likely to flee gossip. You know Donnerville?"

"Slightly."

Blandness instantly swallowed a tiny flicker of disbelief. He said, "They know it can't provide even half the personnel for the Griffith Factories just outside it. It's small enough for a back-fence grapevine, and the tongues are likely wagging yet, as they probably did when Penelope married Harvey fifteen years earlier, and with good cause both times."

"What made the marriage unusual?"

"Even the minister came to the ceremony under the impression he was going to unite Penelope to a garage mechanic names Oscar Ives. She told me, still raging after fifteen years, that Ives sent her a note on their wedding eve stating he intended to join, instead of her, the U.S. Marines, which, incidentally, he did. Possibly because of a disproportion in their respective amplitudes. Her snapshot of him showed a slender young fellow, whereas she was something like —well—an over-blown Kewpie doll. Not unattractive, mind you. I found her features even pretty, although her form was shapely, it was almost monumental, well over two hundred pounds.

"According to her, if your imagination can encompass the image, she rebounded. Actually, it involved little more than submitting to gravity, her apartment being directly over her lunchroom with its one-man chef, waiter, and bus boy, Harvey Matson, who—"

The arrival of Tony with glasses of tomato juice provided an interruption. Lieutenant Carmichael sipped his, widened his eyes and gulped down the remainder.

I smiled. "'Wholesome' is usually so pallid a term applied to food. But here it acquires dimension. You were coming to this Harvey Matson—"

"Probably deep in meditation," he said, "the lunchroom being empty, and solitude having that effect on us. I imagine—"

"Us?" I interrupted.

He indicated my copy of *Lotus Leaves*. "We're not legion, Mister—ah—Smith. Questioning institutionalized clichés is deemed heretical. Not only in America. Everywhere, and always. I was driven to heresy by a broken home. You?"

"Probably through being an orphan," I murmured, causing his head to bob knowingly.

"The same for Harvey Matson! Orphanhood spared him cultural loathing of nonconformity. Being slight and unpre-possessing isolated him from his comic book generation. Poverty limited his sources of refuge. He found a home in the Donnerville Public Library, where I found his intellectual history on withdrawal slips: a brief orgy of fiction before he stumbled on Durant's *Story Of Philosophy*. By fourteen he was groping through Plato. At sixteen he'd renewed Kant's *Critique of Reason* three times—and it hasn't been off its shelf since, by the way. In it I found undisturbed his note claiming Kant's synthetic perceptions poked windows into Leibnitz' monads. Something of a non-sequitur, wouldn't you say?"

"Not to Kant," I shrugged.

His expression softened. "You can't appreciate what a relief it is to discuss this with someone able to follow me.

When I attempt this reconstruction in the Department they look as if I'm talking Choctaw. We must, after this is settled, have some long talks. It will help relieve your monotony."

"What monotony?" I asked.

He sighed unhappily. "The trouble is, just as I've warmed to the abstract image of Harvey Matson, I'm warming to the flesh and blood you, as I would, I suppose, to anyone of a philosophical bent. Physically, he may have been a carbon of you, the antithesis of Penelope. Where she'd stand out in a mob, he'd be lost in a group of three, of two, in fact, if you can believe it."

"I can," I assured him. "I'm frequently ignored in restaurants, sometimes when I'm the only patron."

"I can see why," be said. "I had you in range all the way from the bookshop, yet lost you. But I found it hard to believe that people who'd been served meals by Harvey Matson for ten or fifteen years could recall only that he was small and slender and of pale complexion. No two of them agreed on the color of his eyes. The shape of his nose went unremarked. They could remember no moles or other distinguishing characteristics. For fifteen years he'd been there like a stool, a shelf or some other lunchroom fitting and, like such objects, rarely really seen.

"Even his voice," he said, then paused as Tony set before us platters of breaded veal cutlet and side dishes of baked potatoes and green peas, a salad of black olives, radishes, celery and lettuce hearts, sesame rolls and butter. Lieutenant Carmichael sliced a forkful of cutlet, and halfway to his mouth paused to wave it at me. "Your voice is faint, forcing me to lean a bit to catch your words. Had you been of no prior interest to me, perhaps I wouldn't bother. Donnerville hadn't bothered to listen to Harvey Matson. One literate diner who'd never before given it any thought told me it had been like hearing his own inner voice. As if he might wonder aloud, 'Is the pot roast any good?' then think, 'It certainly is,' and order it. Later, wondering what kind of pie was available, he'd think: Lemon, Cherry, Apple, Blueberry, and so on. Coming to, 'I wonder what's the tab?' and thinking, 'Six thirty-two,' whereupon a ten-dollar bill would vanish from his hand, wherein, as by alchemy, would appear his change. And somehow he would discover himself back in the street, happily fed but with no distinct recollection of having been served; well on his way toward being conditioned for Tomorrow's automation"

"Oh, come!" I protested.

"Do you find the conceit absurd?"

"It's preposterous!"

He nodded as if in confirmation. "I imagine it would have seemed so to Harvey, considering every situation's three basic truths: Yours, Mine, and God's. How Harvey seemed to himself is the crux of my dilemma. How he seemed to the world explained the heist's success. How he seems to himself would determine what steps he has taken since."

Mouthing the cooling forkful of cutlet, his jaw all but quivered. He fell to with astonishing zest. Not until his main and side dishes were polished did he sink back with a contented sigh and resume.

"I imagine my literate informant would have seemed as spectral to Harvey who, while serving him, would be absorbed deep within himself, perhaps with an outward expression such as you have now, weighing whether the transcendental aesthetic successfully retrieved Hume's empiricism from its dead end, a man so self-absorbed that only a violent stimulus could wrench his full attention to external matters—such as the spectacle of the sobbing Penelope, that evening, permitting gravity to convey her some two hundred, albeit proportionate, pounds down the stairway to him.

"She told me he swept her off her feet, if you can credit such a metaphor in this context. But I can. Ives' note had put an aching void in her libido, whereas Harvey's libido had never confronted so amenable a target. The moment contained a symbiotic synthesis of their interlocking needs. When she aired Ives' betrayal, he murmured sympathy. She thanked him for understanding, warming to his denunciation of Ives, as he warmed to her appreciation of his sympathy. You have a crescendoing situation whose momentum alone would find Harvey somewhat in the position of embracing a feather mattress while hot tears rained down on his face and words yielded to lips, a conjunction, I imagine, he discovered akin to the sensation of being swallowed, the which, in fact, transpired legally on the following morning, with the invited witnesses attending."

He regarded me with such inexplicable compassion that I felt color creep into my cheeks. He became aware of the deep-dish apple pies that had materialized before us, and of the steaming cups of black coffee with accompanying containers of cream. Absently he dropped two lumps of sugar into his, poured cream and stirred.

"From what I gathered," he resumed, "the honeymoon lasted the time it took them to walk from the church to the lunchroom. By then, Penelope's emotional pendulum had swung back to indignation. There it seemed to freeze into that fury like which Hell is purported to have none. And for lack of Ives as a target, Harvey served.

"The neighbors, while unable to recall whether his teeth were regular or stained, or even if they were false, recall in detail how he served, the mnemonic being Voice. In contrast to his, Penelope's could rattle walls, and frequently did, spurring Harvey from chore to chore, a process extending through closing hours to domesticity, when Voice rendered their private lives public. It was Harvey who cooked and served their private meals, vacuumed their floors, washed their windows, did their laundry, all the while being reminded of his idleness, venality, avarice, clumsiness, mawkishness and the whole catalogue of husbandly traits wives are prone to compile. Nor does any neighbor recall him once replying in kind, or even replying at all. The general impression was that he loved her, if that can be credited."

"It can," I assured him. "I am drawn irresistibly to large, well-proportioned women. I would recoil at the prospect of embracing one of those barely fleshed skeletons who pass for women in current fashion."

"Is that so? Are you married, Mister—ah—Smith?"

"Separated."

"Is she—?"

"Yes," I said.

"Well, love, I suppose. But consider: Voice driving him through his chores became the sum of his life for fifteen years! Nothing drove Penelope to such fury as discovery of a library volume of Hegel or Santayana he had cached. 'All that Commie propaganda!' was her description of such works to me. And then there was music. He favored modern classics. But Bartok never survived five minutes on the lunchroom radio, the PBS Channel on their TV, or his record player before Voice dictated a turn of dial or replacement of record, the latter to Country Music, the former to a crime program or soap opera, Penelope being addicted to light fiction, especially mystery. She purchased each new paperback thriller as it came out, dragged Harvey to every B-picture. For fifteen years, along with fading memories of Decartes, Spinoza and the like, we can assume his psyche became cluttered with the foibles of cops and robbers, even as his reflexes became conditioned to the trigger of Voice.

"After fifteen years, he must have been more robot than man, an inconspicuous little fellow intensely absorbed in trying, for ex ample to burst the cogito's vicious circle while absently going through the motions of living. One such motion, each weekday morning at nine, was to bring the preceding day's receipts to the Donnerville National for deposit.

"And this was his chore that Friday morning when he was seen leaving the lunchroom, spurred by the injunction neighbors were wont to set their watches by: 'Don't be all day about it, for crying out loud!' He was, as a matter of record, all life about it, never having been seen in Donnerville since."

"Surely at the bank—" I began to say, but swallowed the rest before the impact of Lieutenant Carmichael's intense frown as it loomed through a cloud of bluish smoke. Dessert and coffee having been consumed, he had proffered me a cigar and, scarcely noting my refusal, had ignited one for himself.

"For fifteen years," he said, "he probably existed in the bank, as in the lunchroom, as someone sensed but not really seen. A guard has a fuzzy recollection of colliding with someone entering the bank's revolving door that morning. The guard was en route to another doorway which led to the bank's executive offices. Subsequently, beyond that door, behind a wastepaper basket, was found Harvey's lunchroom deposit.

"It is assumed that the collision with the guard knocked the deposit to a spot on the floor before the guard's moving foot which, moving, kicked it through the doorway, and that Harvey entered the doorway immediately behind the guard in an effort to retrieve it.

"Just inside that doorway, as the guard preceded to the washroom, the bank's manager, Hiram J. Findlay, collided with a vague someone stooping in his path. He recalls helping this person upright and, owing to a chain of coincidental circumstances I'll get to, saying, 'Ah, there you are!'

"Findlay recalls an affirmative reply." Cigar smoke billowed furiously. "Maybe. I doubt it. Expecting affirmation, he would have assumed it had Harvey squeaked, 'What?'

Findlay recalls going on to say, 'You're unobtrusive, all right!' Probably roaring it. He roared all his replies to my queries. He recalls adding, 'It beats me why old Griffith pulls these damn-fool stunts. But it's his funeral. Sign here!'

"Roared, you understand, and in a Voice that well may have had a nostalgic effect on Harvey, probably verging on the hypnotic. At least that's one explanation for his signing the bank receipt, although not why he signed it Findlay! Perhaps he was simply under the misapprehension that had been asked of him.

"But even such intense self-absorption, you would think, might be disturbed when Findlay roared: 'Okay. Get 'em outta here,' then held open the door for Harvey to exit in the possession of two large and heavy suitcases.

"Even assuming reflex to Voice and an almost pathological inner preoccupation, could it be stretched to accommodate a new Voice, that of a cab driver parked outside the Donnerville National, shouting at him: 'Hey, Mac! If you're gonna make the New York Limited, hop in!,' moving Harvey to deposit and follow the two bags into the vehicle? What do you think?"

"Twilight," I murmured, causing the Lieutenant's face to thrust at me through the smoke.

"What's that?"

"Between sleep and wakefulness," I said, "equating such intense self-absorption to sleep. Emerging from it, I imagine you would pass through a sort of twilight zone, much like those few moments you hang suspended between sleep and wakefulness. And if this Harvey was truly of a philosophical turn of mind, even if he idly realized he was committing a crime, one part of his mind would stand aside and watch the remainder of him perform, analyzing the motives, aware, for instance, that no error is trivial, as Freud demonstrated. And this might have served to extend the twilight zone, until Harvey was in the taxi en route to the depot. At which time he may have realized he had passed the point of graceful return. He faced intense, possibly embarrassing interrogation, possibly even imprisonment."

"On the other hand," chimed in Lieutenant Carmichael, "if he simply submitted to events, what could be lose? He'd gain enough wealth to buy a philosophical refuge, stock it with all the philosophy and Bartok he wanted. All he'd lose would be dawn-to-dusk tedium in the lunchroom, around-the-clock nagging from a wife so gross, he—" His eyes popped. He breathed, "I'm dreadfully sorry!"

"Quite all right," I said.

He puffed a thick cloud between us, as if to hide his embarrassment, and spoke rapidly: "Well, it didn't matter that he missed the New York Limited and had to wait twenty minutes for a local. Mark Griffith had not yet sent his 'unobtrusive' agent for that week's payroll due his fifteen thousand employees—nor did he until hours later. And by then Harvey sat behind the bolted door of a small hotel room in mid-Manhattan tearing open paper envelopes and computing a sum just short of one million dollars, a distinction the press and TV did not belabor.

"We found the envelopes next morning, after learning he'd registered as Matthew Harris, indicating that at this stage he was fully committed. I imagine all the cops and robbers claptrap Penelope had spoon-fed his psyche began to yeast. What good disguising his name while his face retained its identity? At eight that evening a Times Square novelty shop transacted business in masquerade devices with a man whose total lack of impression on the salesclerk negatively identifies Harvey.

"That left one further problem. What avail a new face where the old is known? And so, unaware that even Penelope could not furnish us with a description worth putting on a wanted reader, or that the only photograph of him unearthed had been taken at the orphanage when he was ten, showing little more than a blur, he repacked the suitcases, checked out at the hotel's desk, paused in a dimly lit corner of the lobby to apply his purchases, and then—"

"Walked into the arms of a policeman," I interjected, smiling.

A deep sigh escaped Lieutenant Carmichael. He leaned back, as if finally surfeit with examination of my face. Half closing his eyes, he drew on his cigar and said, "An officer named Hershkowitz, who gaped at him and demanded, 'What gives, Mac? You left over from a convention?'

"If not Hershkowitz, it would have been an officer on the next block. Any officer would stop a man carrying two suitcases and wearing an obvious shoulder-length blond wig, a black Groucho mustache, dark blue glasses and a red spider wart on his cheek.

"Hershkowitz told me later, 'It was like the guy turned to jelly.' A good metaphor, considering how the suitcases dropped to the sidewalk. And the right-hand one sprang open—"

"Spewing money," I supplied. "It was well publicized."

Lieutenant Carmichael frowned down at the cigar in his hand, as if trying to identify what it was. "Tipster," he finally said. "There's one in every precinct. Word got around so fast, by the time Harvey was brought in for arraignment, TV cameras were already set up and news photographers overflowed the place, and they were allowed a field day. Before any sort of order could be established, someone asked for shots of Harvey minus the disguise. Imprudently eager uniforms moved in to oblige, removing the blond wig, the Groucho mustache, the dark blue glasses, the red spider wart.

"Back stepped the headline-happy uniforms with their trophies. Cameras were aimed—" Lieutenant Carmichael kept studying his cigar. "I guess you would know better than I how the lenses had difficulty focusing, how they seemed to narrow, widen, squint, gape, possibly even water—until finally someone realized they were seeking a mirage."

"Why me?" I asked.

"Two possibilities confront me," he said musingly, as if I had not spoken. "It could have been that the cameramen jockeying for position, reporters closing in for interviews and patrolmen edging close to get in range of tabloid posterity simply elbowed and squeezed so slight a figure as yourself out of the room. Or possibly you stole away through all that confusion wittingly, having been vouchsafed that flash of self-revelation so few of us attain in our lifetimes, the spectacle of yourself as others saw you—or, in this instance, didn't see you! They certainly didn't as you made your way out of that room, through a long corridor jammed with shortly to be down-graded officers, down the precinct steps and into the night, with close to a hundred thousand—"

"Not me, Lieutenant," I interrupted.

"—Dollars taped to your anatomy, I'd guess," he went on, ignoring my protest. "A wise precaution, anticipating the possibility you may have had to drop the suitcases and run, Mr. Matson. "

"Smith," I corrected him.

"A month later," he went on, ignoring me, "upon my return from Donnerville, I checked the Forty-Second Street Library's records, and soon discovered you'd been looking up volumes of Oriental Philosophy the Donnerville Library lacked. Under alias, of course. But by then I was sufficiently familiar with your script to recognize it through the assorted names you employed. What struck me was all the times you returned to Lee Chin's *Lotus Leaves*. In fact, alongside one parable I found your notation."

"Not mine," I protested.

"About the boy who'd been raised by a mountain hermit in such purity that when the hermit died and the boy wandered off the mountain and into the village in the valley below and saw a bonfire in the village square he stepped into it to warm himself against the valley's chill. The startled villagers shouted for him to jump clear before he burned to death. Curiously, he asked what meant those terms, 'burn' and 'death'. They shouted definitions at him until he finally understood. And the moment he did, he was burned to a crisp."

"Lee Chin's gibe at the Chinese equivalent of Yoga," I said.

"Is that your current view?" he asked, raising troubled eyes to mine. "I thought you deemed it a substantiation of a Yoga premise. Not subscribing to it; the scope of your reading was too broad to have landed you in such a narrow metaphysical byway, but as a sort of oddity. Didn't your notation indicate you likened yourself to Lee Chin's hermit boy, surviving the robbery as he did the flames—until acquisition of vulgar knowledge, the disguises you wore, brought you to heel. And wouldn't your sequel have been removal of the disguises restoring you to a state of exaltation?"

Amused, I could not help asking, "And Lee Chin's sequel should have been that by forcing himself to forget the definitions of 'burn' and 'death' the hermit boy would have become un-burned, as it were, and restored to life?"

"Wasn't that the implication in your notation?"

"Not mine, Lieutenant," I protested.

His ruddy face mirrored great internal agitation. "Believe me, I regret this necessity. I fail to see how your defense could convince a jury, as I am convinced, that the Donnerville National actually robbed itself. Certainly a case could be made for temporary insanity, the legal grounds being inability to distinguish right from wrong—owing to such intense absorption in conflicting philosophical systems as to blur all such ethical distinctions."

"A fascinating point," I said, "but I am not—"

"Of course you are!" he insisted unhappily. "Final identification is inevitable. For now, it suffices you are a slight, pale-complexioned man of faint voice, separated from a large, well-proportioned woman, agreeing Leibniz' monads must be windowless, acquainted with Lee Chin. You claimed to have no knowledge of the matter, saying crime news depressed you, yet you knew precisely at what moment you were arrested. You parade under such an obvious alias as—"

My laughter, erupting beyond my control, cut him short. In a mirth-choked voice I managed to gasp: "But I am Pete Smith! Crime news depresses me ordinarily for its lack of artistry. I am the author of several mystery novels, several hundred magazine stories—all dealing with crime. Here—"

And from various pockets I produced my driver's license, credit cards, two letters. "You claim to be familiar with Matson's script, certainly with his signature. Look—" And, taking my pen, I scrawled on the back of a publisher's letter the name, Harvey Matson, again and again, then flipped the letter over to him, saying, "If this doesn't suffice, we can go around the corner to my apartment where I have lived the past eight years, or to any of several editorial offices, where I have been known even longer, or down to wherever you have Harvey Matson's prints on file, where—"

I stopped then, shocked into pity by the man's transformation. It was as if all the vitality had been drained from him, leaving his face pale and haggard, his body slumped. A palsied hand fumbled the material back across the table to me.

"That would be unnecessary, Mister Smith," he said hoarsely. "You permitted me to go on at such length—gathering material?"

"To be fictionalized," I assured him earnestly.

"I was so certain!" he breathed. "Especially the *Lotus Leaves*—the first copy sold in Manhattan the past eleven months! I was so—" He grew aware of my anxious regard. "Please. If you will summon the waiter—"

"He's here," I said. "But you must allow me the honor. I fear the profit from this encounter has been exclusively mine."

I took the bill from Tony before Lieutenant Carmichael could protest, nor did he, scarcely noting the transaction as he arose heavily and made his slow way out of The Gourmand.

Tony took my twenty-dollar bill and the copy of *Lotus Leaves* I had purchased for him. I told him, "You shouldn't have written out the bill. He's familiar with your handwriting, you know."

"I heard," he replied in a voice so faint it may have been my own inner reflection. It took me a few moments to realize his pale lips were wreathed in a significant smile. "Do you think it would have really mattered, Mister Smith?"

"Well—"

"I see you remain unconvinced," he murmured sadly, then brought my money and his volume back to the kitchen where his enormous wife, albeit a subdued Penelope whose erstwhile Voice had yielded to her worship of Mystery, now embodied in a husband who Had Gotten Away With It, computed my change, taking into account the *Lotus Leaves*' cost.

She had thought of the Forty-Second Street Library first and there had met Harvey on the very day she fled Donnerville gossip.

It would have amazed Lieutenant Carmichael to learn Harvey welcomed her advent, never having resented her decibelic domination, rather appreciating it as an instrument relieving him of the need to deal with superficial trivia at the price of his pre-occupation.

And this only incidentally involved the monumental abstractions attributed to him by Lieutenant Carmichael. Actually it concerned the Yoga, which the Lieutenant had deemed an incidental oddity.

According to the man I knew as "Tony", what enabled him to emerge from the Law's hands unscathed had been a supra-natural self-mastery which enabled him to melt from the sight of ordinary mortals. Had not his endless hours of Yoga-incantation achieved as much before—all the times he had been walked into by people whose astonishment at his materialization was expressed in a "Sorry! I didn't see you!" Hence his unconcern about whether or not Lieutenant Carmichael recognized his handwriting on the bill. "Tony" was convinced he simply could have "vanished" again.

In the Donnerville taxicab, where realization of his predicament first intruded itself upon his Yoga incantations, he had rejected the idea of returning in favor of the idea that so large a sum would prove useful toward furthering his projected research. The bank's loss, he reasoned, would be made up by insurance companies who, in turn, would recover their loss by a minuscule hike in rates. In a population of two hundred million, he estimated that to be a fraction of a cent per person, a bagatelle to History's wealthiest citizenry—particularly when its employment would prove so valuable to mankind. For he envisaged developing further supra-natural talents, defying gravity, for instance, as Tibetan Lamas reputedly could, and eventually, through publication, to make such wonders accessible to all.

Not properly a philosopher, you see, despite all the epistemology he waded through—actually to pluck what he could from context to substantiate the escapist compulsion sparked initially by a migratory charlatan's leaflet he read in the orphanage, and which saddled and rode him since. He was more psychopath than philosopher.

What prevented me from exposing him after recognizing who he actually was (probably because we were of a type—and, as children say, it takes one to know one) was his unaccountably superb cookery. And his prices, while not outlandish, were still high enough to scare away the less discriminating, leaving The Gourmand a perfect haven where I could dine upon wholesome viands in the genteel atmosphere I require to free my imagination for the pursuit of the plot intricacies necessary to my work.

As selfish a rationalization as was his in absconding with the bank's money, I concede, and one that troubled me slightly as I emerged from The Gourmand and was all but knocked flat by the onrushing Lieutenant Carmichael.

His face inflamed, his eyes burning wildly, he helped me roughly to my feet, muttering, "Didn't think you'd come out with *Lotus Leaves*! Bought it for him, didn't you?" Without awaiting my reply, he explained: "I'd gone five blocks before it struck me—what that diner had told me in jest—how he'd emerge from Harvey Matson's lunchroom, fed, but with no distinct recollection of having been served!"

Whereupon he released me and plunged into The Gourmand.

I continued to my apartment, heavy of foot and heart, knowing that in this huge city I would never again find a dining refuge so perfectly suited to my needs.

Erroneously, of course. You may have seen the next day's headline:

PHANTOM CROOK ESCAPES AGAIN!

the deal

MARK, the greyed headwaiter of the Jamamba Supper Room, leaned over the tanned young man.

"Doctor Brown, Mr. Dudley would like to see you upstairs in his office."

Doctor Brown smiled helplessly at the young lady seated across from him. "Mind?"

No, her eyes indicated. Her eyes were large, dark and tilted slightly at the outer corners. Along with her high cheekbones, coal black hair brought to a knot behind and her rosebud lips, they made her seem almost Asian. What the remainder of her did to a black satin dress tugged at men's eyes throughout the Supper Room.

Finest looking couple he had seen in a month, Mark thought, and sighed.

"I'll be just a few minutes," the doctor said, smiling, watching for acknowledgment in those almost Asian eyes, and getting it.

In Mark's wake he wended through a sea of chewing, sipping, talking faces, skirted the small dance floor hosting half a dozen couples convulsing to a combo's agitated beat and followed Mark through swinging doors which shut silently behind him, then up a stairway.

At the head of it two large men in evening clothes flanked double doors from behind which issued a genteel hum of voices and the sharper sounds of ivory balls bouncing on slowly revolving surfaces.

Further along this upper landing two large man in evening clothes opened a single door at their approach. Mark nodded the young doctor in, then retraced his steps down to the bar where Henri, who had been head bartender as long as Mark had been head waiter, cocked an inquiring brow.

Mark shrugged slightly, then moved off to greet new arrivals.

Within the upstairs office, behind a large teakwood desk, sat a toad-shaped man whose pink face surrounded a fat, unlit cigar. He motioned to a pale leather armchair that matched a pale leather divan against the far wall.

"Put it there, Doc."

The doctor sat.

"No use beatin' around the bush," Dudley said past his unlit cigar. "I hold your markers for near a hundred grand, and it's beginnin' to look like a long cold Winter. I okayed your markers 'cause I figgered how docs charge nowadays you'd have no trouble makin' it up. But I checked you since. You're set up in a little clinic down the East Side. Welfare Blacks. Puerto Ricans. Haitians. Jamaicans—" The cigar was plucked from its soft nest and employed in a deprecatory gesture "—that kind of crap. It'll be a hell of a lot of Winters before you could ante up that hundred G's. So I gotta get it outta you some other way, see?"

"Frankly, Mr. Dudley, I don't."

"Well—" the cigar poised erect "—I lead a dry life, Doc. Dough means little. Food? Whatever fills me'll do. Turn-ons like hootch 'n dope leave me cold. Gamblin' is just arithmetic. Culture shit goes over my head. I gotta go a long way for kicks. See?"

"Not really-" the young doctor began, only to be silenced by a gesture.

"Then there's dames," Dudley said, his voice caressing the noun. "Was a time I flipped over 'em. Any size, shape, color. As long as they could wiggle." The cigar began rolling back and forth between the soft lips again. "Nowadays it's tough an' gettin' tougher. Any dame I can have I don't want. Up to a couple years back, if it was a question of relief I'd phone Sally Romance t'send up whatever I thought I wanted. It got so I made out better playin' with myself."

The doctor watched his host's small eyes glaze thoughtfully.

"Then there's the dames I can't have." The cigar became motionless again. "You ever feel it, Doc? Walk down a street an' it's like electricity. A totally strange dame you have time for just one fast look at?" The cigar sagged. "Next second she's out of sight an' you feel like, hell, like you missed the chance of a lifetime. Get what I'm drivin' at?"

"No."

"You will. The first time was about two years ago. This guy flopped on my tables even bigger than you. Owned a chain of stores. But when it came time to collect, it turned out he was goin' into Chapter Eleven, with back taxes about to eat up whatever he had left. Came in to work out a deal. Didn't know the dame with him was his wife, but like that hot flash stuff in the street, one look at her in that—" Following the cigar's gesture, Doctor Brown turned to look behind him and saw, on the far wall over the pale leather divan, a large color television screen which happened, at that moment, to be focused on the exotic-looking woman he had left below in the Supper Room. "One look," said Dudley, bringing the doctor's attention around again, "and I was jelly. So help me, I sat here shakin' like a leaf! Then he came in here to work out a deal and I put it to him straight. Turned out the lady was his wife. Later, I brought his markers right down to their table and they both tore 'em up. That was after he'd talked her into comin' up here an' spendin' half an hour alone with me."

The young doctor stared.

Dudley shrugged. "I forget how many times it happened since. Couple of times I got a solid *'No!'* and hadda collect the old way. Some of these came around in time. A few got up the dough. Only once I missed all around. The guy took his lickin' and kept his sister to hisself. From bank vice-president to door-to-door brush salesman in one easy step! The ones that went along—" The cigar grew rigid. "—can't put in words how great it is! The kind of dames I'd never been able to even talk to before! They didn't like any part of it, but they liked whoever sent 'em up enough to force themselves. An' when I got 'em on that couch, I can't tell you how absolutely terrific it was every time! So that's how I get my kicks these days, Doc."

Doctor Brown kept staring at the soft pink face. Dudley's gaze dropped to the unlit cigar now rolling back and forth between his stubby fingers.

"Then there's you, Doc. Almost a hundred grand in markers, but no way you can go to a judge an' pass 'em off as gamblin' debts you don't have to pay. Legitimate Promissory Notes. And then I found out you're payin' off over eighty grand in bank loans for the equipment in your clinic. But you never told that bank you had an almost hundred grand loan outstanding. See? I ain't got much pressure on you. Maybe just enough to put you on the street with no more credit, an' flat broke."

"I see," the doctor breathed.

"Maybe, Doc," murmured Dudley, watching the cigar twirl in his fingers. "I don't need cash. I need kicks. Sometimes I pay high for 'em. Even a hundred grand. That's what I was thinkin' to myself when I looked up at that screen an' saw you come in with that knockout. One quick look an' everythin' inside me went outta control. Doc, is it worth a hundred grand to you to help me get my control back?"

The young doctor came out of his chair slowly. Behind him he heard the door click open. Over his shoulder he saw the large man in evening clothes shutting the door behind him. It was too coincidental, the doctor thought. Dudley must have signaled, probably by way of a floor pedal.

"Take it easy, Doc," Dudley said. "We're only talkin'. I don't care she's your girl, your wife, your sister, or what. Turn me down if you want. I don't know how much treatin' them East Side losers at cut rates means t'you. But turn me down, I'll go after my hundred grand the hard way. Business an' pleasure; that's my story. It's your move, Doc."

Mark and Henri exchanged significant glances when Doctor Brown appeared through the swinging doors. His face was expressionless as he skirted the dance floor and made his way back to his table. Henri made a slight gesture, showing five fingers. Mark's grey head nodded slightly. Henri showed ten fingers. Mark smiled and nodded again. Thereafter, from separate parts of the Supper Room each kept an eye on the tableau at the doctor's table.

The young doctor spoke low, earnestly. She listened without changing expression, her lovely, almost Asian face thoughtfully studying his.

And then occurred what neither Mark nor Henri could understand. Their hands met briefly alongside the table in a perfunctory handclasp. Following which the girl arose and turned in one fluid motion, then walked gracefully toward the swinging doors, her lovely head poised high. Mark, standing unobtrusively near the swinging doors, studied her face from the corners of his shock-filled eyes. Her expression was sleepily serene. She swept by him and he became engulfed by a wave of exotic perfume as the doors swung shut behind her.

"Well, *mon ami*?" Henri's cynical smile materialized at his elbow.

Unseen by others in the Supper Room a ten-dollar bill passed from Mark's hand to Henri's.

"I'd have bet a hundred he wouldn't have allowed it!" Mark sighed.

"I wish you would have," replied Henri dryly.

"How could I have misjudged him so?" Mark brooded.

"I bet on the woman," Henri shrugged. "The lure was too strong."

"The lure of that *toad* upstairs?" Mark snorted.

Henri regarded him affectionately. "You'll never understand women, *mon ami*. They all dream secretly at one time or another about wallowing in a cave with an ape. And here it's tied in with romance—sacrificing themselves for the man they love. Add to that being valued at many tens of thousands of dollars for just a few minutes of their time. And top it with how they'll be able to use it as a club anytime the man steps out of line. Damn few women could resist such an opportunity!"

Mark sighed. "I bet on *him*! I would have trusted him with my daughter!"

"Once he told her about it, *mon ami*, the decision became hers. I'll always bet on a woman to do the worst, if she can feel noble doing it!"

They watched in silence as a waiter set a fresh Scotch highball before the young doctor. Several highballs later, from different parts of the room they watched Dudley sink his toad-shaped hulk onto the chair the girl had vacated.

"She said to tell you goodnight," Dudley said.

Doctor Brown nodded.

Dudley produced a packet of documents from a jacket pocket and placed them before the doctor. He watched as the tanned fingers tore them into halves, then quarters, then did the same to each quartered section, and continued the process until they were little more than a pile of confetti.

"We even, Doc?"

The doctor nodded, curiously studying the slack features before him. Dudley's breath was short, his pink face coated with perspiration. Purplish bags had appeared below his protruding eyes. His voice seemed to have grown hoarser.

"All my life—" the cigar in his soft lips trembled, "—nothin' like her ever happened to me. Told you I didn't care what she was to you, but it's drivin' me nuts. It wasn't even five minutes after you walked outta my office she walked in. How could you argue her into it so quick?"

"She is not my girl," Doctor Brown said quietly, "or my wife, my sister, or my what. Did she speak to you?"

The haggard pink face shook from side to side. "Just walked in an' straight up to me an'—keerist!"

"A dull conversationalist," the young doctor shrugged, "but a lovely decoration across a table. I brought her here for that and to brighten her drab life a bit."

Dudley frowned. "You're strandin' me on base, Doc. All I'm askin' is how'd you get her to come up so fast?"

"Quite simply," Doctor Brown said, rising and looking down into the yellowish eyes bulging up at him. "I gave her two hundred dollars."

"Huh?"

"Her usual fee, Mr. Dudley. One of Sally Romance's latest

call girls I've been treating for a complex case of genital herpes and syphilis."

Two objects appeared on the white tablecloth simultaneously. A saliva-coated cigar. And a neat rectangle of pasteboard.

"My address and office hours," Doctor Brown said quietly. "You'll probably want to see me professionally in about ten days."

Then he turned and walked out of the Jamamba Supper Room.

shock performances

THE DOCTOR EMERGED from the bedroom after examining my wife Valerie, and told me: "Ran across a feature article about you in the paper the other day, Johnny. They called you Manhattan's hermit."

"Did they spell my name right?" I smiled.

"Seriously, Johnny, is it true you never—?"

"Been out of Manhattan? Almost, Doc. I spent one summer on a farm as a kid. One summer of mosquitoes in my ears, manure on my shoes, sun blisters on my neck, and work blisters on my hands. A horse kicked me. A cow stepped on my foot. I was only eight, but I made up my mind then that my future would be confined to the asphalt and air conditioning of Manhattan. What lies between Coney Island and Grant's Tomb, the Statue of Liberty and the Bronx Zoo is world enough for me. Why?"

"Does Valerie feel the same way about it?"

"She never complains."

"Of course not," the Doc murmured. "But—"

He let it hang as we gazed down from the apartment at the

nylons twinkling up and down Fifty-seventh Street, until I prompted: "But what, Doc?"

"A few more weeks of Manhattan would kill her," he said.

I gripped hid shoulder and spun him to face me. After all, it was sudden. Just a routine family check-up. For a moment, I didn't believe him.

"This on the level, Doc?"

He nodded solemnly. "A sudden loud noise might do it. Worry. In fact, almost any emotional disturbance. Even—" He went on to describe the type of things that could stand between a heartbeat and eternity. He put it in technical language, then brought it down to my level. Valerie's heart. It needed rest and quiet. "What it would take, Johnny, is a peaceful cottage somewhere in the country. But—"

"No buts!" I snapped. "She goes to the country!"

"You know she can't go alone."

I thought about that and he watched me think about it, until I nodded. "Okay, Doc. *We* go to the country. Pick a spot."

"What about the picture, Johnny?"

"Let Bernstein find another ham. We'll go to any spot you pick, Doc. Make it quick!"

That grin he'd been hiding behind his teeth leaked through and he pumped my hand as if he wanted my vote.

"I already have the spot, Johnny."

"I've been jobbed!" I grinned back at him.

Grin? I could have *howled*! But the doc couldn't know about that. He couldn't hear my heart beat a raucous, triumphant tattoo against my ribs.

After he left, I entered the bedroom and told Valerie all about it. "We're going to the country. We're gonna make like rubes, Hon."

Valerie said, "I know, Johnny." She said it through a mouthful of nougat, the slivery curlers among the broom straws she wears for hair, the pasty lard sagging on her arms, the smear of cold cream on her face running into lipstick and chocolate smears around that perpetually moving mouth; not to mention the extra chins quivering, and cheeks bulging as she chain-ate nougats from the open box at her elbow. She didn't even glance up from her comic book to answer me, this delectable wife of mine. She murmured through nougat: "I know, Johnny. We'll need money. Bring me my checkbook."

I brought her the checkbook.

Did I thank the doc for helping me out of my contract? Bernstein was going to have me, until the doc spoke to him. Then Bernstein practically crawled into my dressing room before my last performance.

I'll have to spring the news to Sheila cold. She's the B-girl in the picture. All the animals on the street dwell on the profile under her chin. I'd defy them to look into her eyes and listen to her voice. Then think of *Valerie*... and try to keep from *retching*.

One night, over cheap wine and dim lights, Sheila put it to me straight. I looked into her eyes and she said, "You're what I want, Johnny, but you're a long time picking up the option."

"Don't commercialize us, Shelia," I pleaded. "You know Valerie. You know what kind of evidence rates a divorce in this state."

"All I know is I want you to stop crowding me into a back street, Johnny."

I reached across the table for her hand.

"A little more patience, Shelia, then I promise you the big contract!"

Her hand avoided mine. She rose from the table. "That's a

broken record. Let's pick this up again when it's clean, shall we, Johnny?"

What could I tell her? That nothing short of murder could wipe this slate clean? I sat there alone at the table and thought of the doc's words and thought of Valerie... and Shelia... and thought how no detective in the whole wide world could lift a fingerprint from a voice...

Valerie's eyes squinted up into the sudden light. "Johnny?" I watched her knuckle her eyes, blink toward the shadowy corner of the room, then turn back to me. I saw the eyes widen at the carving knife gripped in my right hand. "Johnny, what's wrong?" she whispered.

I stood there and watched her come up on one elbow, her eyes flicking uncertainly between the blade and my face.

She tried to sit up. Her face got into the palm of my free hand. I forced her back down to the pillow. I sat at her side and poised the tip of the blade a hairbreadth from her throat.

"They say it doesn't hurt," I told her quietly. "They say you don't even feel the blade sliding in. Just a faint prickle—then peace. You need peace, Valerie. You need to give *me* peace, so I could bring peace to Shelia. But you don't even know about Shelia, do you, Valerie?"

Her eyes screamed at me.

I told her about Shelia. I told her about herself. I told her about her checkbook. I told her in painstaking detail and allowed fury to mount in my voice and hate to etch itself on my face and spasms to twitch my fingers on the haft of the knife. I watched the fear crescendoing in her eyes until the terror that trembled the fat on her face was a wild ugly thing.

Then I sprang to my feet with the knife poised high.

She scampered off the bed and waddled backwards until

the wall held her firm and my blade was a darting shimmer under her eyes.

Words bubbled through her lips.

"Johnny I've got to tell you—"

The expression in her eyes clicked off, leaving them blank.

She crumpled to the floor.

I raised her wrist. Limp. I thumbed back an eyelid. Glossy. I put my ear to her breast; the only thing I heard was the arhythmic pounding of my own heart.

That was when I called the doc again. "It's Valerie," I said. "Get over here quickly. I think she's... dead."

I broke the connection before he could reply because the elation would have forced a roar of triumph through my lips. Hadn't I just committed the perfect murder? Could they raise a fingerprint from my vocal chords? Could they drag my words, expressions, and gestures before a jury and say: 'With these weapons he murdered his wife!'?

I broke the connection and turned from the phone. From the bedroom doorway Valerie said: "What I've been trying to tell you, Johnny-"

That was when my chest exploded and the whole world blurred, until the doc's face swam into focus.

Sure it hurts. It hurts like crazy. But I understand now. The doc knew about that. He knew I'd never leave Manhattan for myself, so he and Valerie cooked up that lie about *her* heart being weak. If I wouldn't leave for myself, maybe I'd leave for her. They couldn't have known...

I can already see the headline for tomorrow's edition:

"The hermit finally came out of his cave... feet first."

Her voice emerged tinnily from my call box. "This is Elaine Howell. May I see you?"

God no, I thought, then watched my finger touch the button to buzz open the building's front door for her six flights below.

Freud could have explained it. I was too hot and exhausted to give it a second thought. I returned to the living room and stared at the phone.

It remained silent. They were having trouble locating Inspector Quinn at this hour. I turned the report I had spent ten evenings writing for him face down on the table, then went to open a window to get some air circulating, and became spattered by fat drops. My drapes billowed past me.

I shut the window and found my face in streaming glass. The flattened nose I got back at the St. Mary's Orphanage. Scar-tissued brows from my teens, fighting neighborhood wolves off my foster sister.

I left my face in the window as the buzzer sounded. Elaine Howell handed me her yellow plastic raincoat and hood with a tired nod, then walked into the living room and stopped in her tracks, looking down at Friday's Early Bird edition of the news in my easy chair.

Another wrinkle for Freud. I should have hidden it before she arrived. Now I could only watch her stare down at her husband glowering up at her from the front page under the caption:

AWAITS EXECUTION

She took up the paper and sank into the chair. I followed her eyes to my mantel clock. 4:07.

"How much longer?" she breathed.

"They usually do it around seven. Don't think about it."

"I've been walking in the rain for hours," she said, "trying to make up my mind whether or not to see you. I finally phoned headquarters, but they wouldn't give me your address. I found it in the phone book."

"I'm glad you came," I said, feeling glad, knowing I wasn't. Heads or tails. It no longer mattered. I asked, "Coffee?"

"Please. Without sugar. Black."

I left her looking down at her husband's sullen scowl in her lap as I brought her dripping raincoat to hang in the bathroom, then entered my kitchen and started the cold water running.

Rain beating on the window in soft staccato was like the muted roll of drums before the daredevil dove off the high board into a tiny net. But there was no daredevil this morning.

Just Oscar J. Howell, scheduled at seven to dive into eternity from a wired chair. His picture in her lap, taken just after the verdict, was accurate. By then his expression had settled permanently into the bitter lines the camera caught.

Not bitter when I first studied him, standing between

uniformed officers in his own office. Answering Sergeant Mattrock's interrogation, he had been argumentative, his smile quick.

Quite a smile, with his white teeth, wiry red hair and the freckles punctuating his neat features. Medium sized, well preserved, clad smartly in light grey, he looked the model for a poster of the ideal American Boy—twenty years after.

"Make him?" Inspector Quinn growled in my ear.

He had drawn me apart from the investigatory confusion after noticing me emerge from the office closet with a white linen jacket.

I watched Howell's pale blue eyes hit and run. Mattrock's bland face. Plainclothesman Cohen's shorthand pad. The sprawled corpse being photographed on the office floor. I shook my head.

"Ozzie Howell. Society bum. Mama's widow of the toothpaste Howell. Been quiet the last three-four years. Before that he was in and out the precincts like he got caught in a revolving door. Brawling over dames. A real loudmouth. Let the sight of Martin reach his belly, he'll fall apart."

On the door's frosted glass could be read backwards:

MARTIN & HOWELL
INVESTMENTS

Quinn followed my glance. "One dead, the other due. When they pull the slug from Martin's head, have it matched to the revolver we took from Howell. That's your case."

"Mine?"

He gripped my bicep. "You got a way with loudmouths, Pete. Mattrock's catchin' your style. Listen—"

The linen jacket held nothing of interest. I tossed it to Patrolman Rosselli, who looked idle, then listened to Howell tell Mattrock: "Jack didn't particularize over the phone. He said something important came up and I should rush over here, even if it meant missing my plane."

"What plane?"

"For Bermuda. My, well..." Howell's quick smile flashed. "Sort of a belated honeymoon. I'd been too busy for one when I was married last month, and—"

"Busy doing what?" Howell's smile grew strained. He shrugged. "What we do—did. Real Estate. Investments—"

"Catch the offbeat?" Quinn whispered as Mattrock provided a pause Howell seemed reluctant to fill. I nodded.

He muttered, "Some business. Practically no outgo in their account at Chemical. But enough comin' in for each of 'em to have paid over a half million taxes on reported income last year. Almost as much the year before. Somethin' eh?"

I nodded and turned back to Howell saying, "Jack was on the floor where he is now when I came in. But not shot. Unconscious. His cheeks—"

He sucked air as his gaze found Martin's cheek. The photography over, a man from the Medical Examiner's office was slicing a powder stained sliver of it into a glass jar.

Martin never could have modeled a poster—unless the before in hair-restorer or weight-reducing ads. Balding and bloated, gold teeth glinted between slightly parted lips. His fingernails and shirt collar seemed grimy, his brown suit threadbare.

"Close guy with a buck," Quinn muttered, following my gaze. "Almost a grand in his wallet. Tended bar at the old Night Owl Club. We caught him one time, eleven years back. Got a suspended."

"For what?"

His face creased into a leathery grin. "Procurin'. Gives it a complexion, eh?"

I nodded and turned back to Howell explaining, "I

thought Jack was sick. I leaned over to shake him" His laugh this time was incredulous. "The next thing, I was waking up on the floor near him. His face was like it is now. Talk about your shocks—"

"Talk about yours," Mattrock prodded gently. "You fainted?"

"No—I was hit. Someone waiting behind the door, probably. I remember stooping over Jack and hearing a faint movement behind me. The next thing, I was on my hands and knees, looking at Jack. That cop was knocking. I was that groggy when I went to unlock the door for him, I didn't realize I was holding Jack's gun—until he took it away from me. That cop. Schiff."

"Who locked the door in the first place?"

"We kept it locked most times. Jack liked to carry large sums. I probably did it automatically."

"Go back a little," Mattrock said. "See anybody as you came in?"

"Only Jack."

"I mean before that."

"The porter. Pop. He was mopping the corridor."

"That's what Pop says," Mattrock said. "He says he heard the shot a few moments later. He banged the door, asking if there was trouble. You hear him?"

"That must have been after I was struck down."

"Somebody heard him," Mattrock said dryly. "When he tried the knob, he heard somebody turn the lock from the inside. He asked a girl in the office across the hall to call us, then remained outside your door, seeing nobody leave or enter, until Patrolman Schiff arrived. Schiff saw no third person when you opened for him. Just you holding the revolver, and Martin dead on the floor behind you, but he didn't search. He remained in the doorway until we arrived. We found nobody hiding. Who could have slugged you?"

"I tell you, somebody—"

"That door is the only way in or out," Mattrock said reasonably. "It's been under observation from the moment you entered—at which time, according to both you and Pop, no shot had been fired."

"Any second now," Quinn growled in my ear as Howell pushed nervous fingers through his hair.

"It sounds crazy the way you tell it," Howell muttered. "It sounds impossible. But I tell you there had to be a third—"

His breath caught. He leaned his red head toward Mattrock, one index finger pointing. "Here," he almost shouted. "I told you! Go ahead, feel it!"

I caught Mattrock's eye, stepped between them. My fingers edged Howell's away from a small lump a bit behind his right ear.

Mattrock said, "This is Lieutenant Burt."

Howell, slowly coming erect, gave no sign of hearing him. He was breathing as if at the end of a long run, the color flooding his freckled cheeks.

I had Mattrock hand me the souvenir baseball bat lying atop one of the two desks. Howell's dazed stare followed it over my head. I watched his eyes jump as I slammed it down on myself with enough force to splay my knees.

Only Quinn's low chuckle broke the startled silence.

I returned the bat to Mattrock and caressed my aching head until I was able to lean it toward Howell and tell him, "It's your turn. Feel mine."

Color abandoned his cheeks leaving each freckle etched as if it had been pasted on.

"Feel it," I said.

His head trembled a negative, in his expression the realization, shared by every man in that office, that he was practically dead.

"Can't understand it," Quinn growled later. "Mama's Boy. A loud mouth. He should have bust wide open."

But he didn't. We got nothing else out of him, then or later. His expression took on the bitter lines that characterized him since, through his trial, and to the front page of the newspaper on his wife's lap in my living room.

Her eyes opened. "Thinking of electrocution," she murmured. "Does it hurt?"

"Possibly for a fraction of a second. Like being struck by lightning."

"I read somewhere they writhe against their straps."

"Reflex. They don't feel it."

"Like a frog's leg kicking when you apply electricity?"

"Something like that. Don't think about it."

Our eyes met returning from the clock. 4:29. Hers shied away. "I'll be all right, Peter. Go tend the coffee."

I stared at her pale, delicate profile a few moments, then bore its impression back to the kitchen. My fingers shook plugging in the percolator. She had never before called me Peter.

But she had been able to shake me ever since Inspector Quinn beckoned me from a precinct basement room where I was interrogating a teenaged stabber a few weeks after Howell's arraignment. He said, "Howell's wife is up on the second floor, waitin' to see who's in charge. You won't believe it. She looks just like that gal you brought to the Benefit. Emily?"

"Betty. That was two benefits ago, Inspector. She died."

His shaggy features softened. "I'm at the age where the years all roll together, Pete. I didn't know."

"Howell's wife?"

"Elaine. You won't believe it. A bum like him, you'd

expect some disco tramp." His head shook. He mauled my shoulder. "Go see her, you'll see. Upstairs in the corridor—"

Quinn wasn't kidding. From behind, Howell's wife was so much like Betty I almost missed a step. Then she turned and the differences steadied me. Younger. More poised. And her voice, when she spoke, was keyed lower.

"Thank you for seeing me, Lieutenant. I was advised not to come. But it's as much your duty to establish innocence as guilt, isn't it?"

"However the evidence points, Mrs. Howell."

"Can't it be wrong?" She asked it breathlessly, adding: "I took a criminology course in Sarah Lawrence. They cited cases in which suspects were ultimately cleared despite over-whelming evidence against them." She turned pink. "Lec-turing you on criminology. I feel so darn sophomoric!"

She was. And innocent. And vulnerable. About twenty-one: a petit brunette whose pert features enhanced tremen-dous eyes. She stood breathlessly erect in trim brown tailoring, the high neck of a pink blouse lacy about her neck, poising her head proudly. Only her slender fingers, continuously kneading her brown eyes bespoke tension.

I said, "Evidence can be invalidated by new evidence."

"I know," she said eagerly. She dug into the purse and produced a crumpled snapshot. "This was taken from Oscar with his other effects when he was arrested."

A dark-haired girl smiling prettily into the camera from the lawn of a ranch-style house. Fragments of city skyline loomed in the distant background.

"I remember it," I nodded, returning it to her. "It was in his hip pocket."

"Not when he left for the office that morning, Lieutenant. I know, because Oscar had put on a new suit for our trip to Bermuda and I handed him everything from the pockets of the suit he had worn the day before. But not this picture. I would have remembered out of jealousy, if for no other reason. The girl looks so alive—"

I waited.

Her flush returned. "I feel such a fool," she murmured. "It seemed so significant when they gave it to me at the police station. But Oscar would have called your attention to it if it was significant. Did he?"

"No, Mrs. Howell."

She smiled wryly. "I'm sorry I'm being ridiculous—"

"You're not," I said gently.

Her smile grew warm. "I know much hinges on that porter's testimony, and that his statement bore up under a lie detector. Does that rule out all possibility that he lied?"

"Not all, Mrs. Howell."

"Then if I find someone profiting from Mr. Martin's death, someone linked to that porter—"

She waited expectantly.

"*We* couldn't," I said. "Not even an heir. What we know is that 'Martin' was an alias he adopted before his prints were ever recorded. But that's it. We found no enemies. Nor friends. Just a few casual acquaintances. He went his own way, minding his own business, whatever it was. Whatever it was, he can no longer tell us. Your husband won't."

She frowned. "Oscar won't tell me, either. I thought he was evading taxes and trying to protect me, But he's so stubborn about it, even with his lawyers. I think it must go deeper. His mother's quite wealthy and possessive, you know?"

"I heard."

"He kept trying to break away, ran wild when he was younger. But you probably know about that."

That and her. Psychology now. If she found him eating the neighbor's baby raw, it wouldn't be rampant cannibalism —but the effect of a trauma inflicted by his mother pretending to nibble his toes when he was a baby. She was breaking my heart.

I said, "Yes, Mrs. Howell."

"She gave him a fantastic allowance. And you probably know how attractive he is to women—"

I knew. I nodded.

"Which you probably resent," she went on, flushing again, but returning my stare levelly, "because you...well, I'm not trying to bait you, Lieutenant. A plain man being jealous of an attractive one is only natural. I mention it so you will recognize it in yourself should it subtly influence your reaction to new evidence which may prove favorable to him. If I wrong you, forgive me."

"It's okay," I breathed.

"I feel you're honest," she continued, her cheeks blazing. "I have good instincts about people, aside from having majored in Psychology at Sarah Lawrence. I feel your honesty as strongly as I feel Oscar's innocence."

Thanking her, forgiving her, overwhelmed by her, I managed a nod.

She became brisk. "So keeping his business secret, even from me may be an extension of that same rebellion against his mother, a compulsion to be his own man. But their business is the logical place to seek whoever profited from Mr. Martin's death, isn't it?"

Whatever she saw in my face filled hers with compassion. She touched my arm. "I hurt you, Lieutenant, didn't I? I was thoughtless. I'm so very sorry—"

I shook my head, forcing a wry grin. "They called me 'The Gargoyl' in college."

"It's an honest, decent face," she said gently. "Whatever information I bring, I know you will treat it dispassionately." She grew aware of her hand tight on my bicep, let it drop to her side, turning crimson again. She whispered, "Goodbye for now, Lieutenant."

I watched her walk swiftly to the stairway, then down it and out of sight.

Quinn materialized at my elbow. "Didn't I tell you, Pete?"

I nodded.

"Shows the power of proximity. Her folks lived across the road from his Mama, in Bronxville. And they say he's got it, whatever gets 'em."

"I just heard," I breathed.

Quinn grunted. "He stand a chance?"

I shook my head.

"That lousy bum," Quinn growled. "I'm for fryin' him even if it turns out he's innocent, which it won't, just to keep him from clutterin' up that kid's life. You sure he's cooked?"

"Positive."

"She'll give it a battle anyhow. Right up to the last second. Watch."

A week later, I watched her enter my office with a list of apartments found within a jacket lining while packing Howell's clothes for storage during her move from their Gracie Square duplex to a West Side furnished room.

Forty-eight apartments in as many buildings scattered throughout the city, with tenant's name and a money entry alongside each. The lowest was rated: $1,248.00, the highest: $26,759.56.

"I don't know what it means," she said, taking the list back from me. "I learned all these apartments are in buildings owned by a Barker Corporation, but nobody there ever heard of Mr. Martin or my husband. Oscar grew angry when I told him about it. He told me to burn the list." Hurt showed in her enormous eyes. "He's so irritable about everything. That I sold our Cadillac and my jewelry to finance our case. And he said I should burn that picture you found in his pocket. He was furious that I talked to you."

I stared at her thoughtful frown.

"Why should he be so reluctant to help me? Even if the business was unethical—"

"How?" I breathed.

"Gambling. Bootlegging—" Her head shook impatiently. "Whatever. But how could exposure of it hurt him any more than he stands to be hurt now?"

I could offer no more than a faint shrug. She said, "At four of these addresses they slammed the door in my face. Would you go back with me?"

I paused to collect a packet of police photographs, then accompanied her to a Yorkville address with a $2,457.87 notation alongside it. The list's tenant, matching the name in the doorbell slot, was Alice Smith who opened the door wide enough to show me only a bloodshot eye under a platinum crest. The eye dipped to my wallet shield, arose to my face.

"Lieutenant Burt," I said, leaning on the door. It widened enough for me to glimpse a blur of flesh scurrying rearward. I looked down into the now two bloodshot eyes of the chemical blonde. "Your name and address came up on a list involved in a homicide, Miss Smith. It is Miss Smith?"

Her reply was in a brandy baritone. "Gotta warrant?"

"You can answer me here or down headquarters."

"How'd I get on a list?"

"That's my first question."

"Well, you're in," she shrugged, releasing the door, then sighted Elaine Howell following and screeched: "You again!"

Being in, if only technically, I brushed past her effort to slam the door. Behind a rear door was a female voice shrill with excitement. I flung it open and managed to wrest free the receiver from a hand as weak as a child's.

Redhead. Eighteen or nineteen, she wore a vague expression featuring a broad splash of crimson across her lips, and absolutely nothing between that and red sandals.

"I already told Nickie," she giggled, trying to focus on me with bloodshot eyes.

The receiver held only dial hum. I cradled it, told the girl, "Put something on. You'll catch cold," then re-entered the living room where Elaine Howell had the blonde's thin wrists under control.

Both were panting, Elaine Howell's eyes enormous on the flimsy black net garment that clung to Alice Smith like a transparent layer of skin. Tiny scarlet hearts decorated the net in lieu of fig leaves.

"Take it easy," I murmured, wedging between them, looking down into the chemical blonde's outraged eyes.

"Bustin' in here!" she panted.

"On your invitation," I reminded, producing my packet of full faces and profiles. I fanned them slowly before her. "Know any of these men?"

Her scowl lowered to the pictures. A peroxide thirty. A caricature of seductiveness in the harsh noonlight flooding that ivory-hued room. She tapped one picture with a finger whose nail was the color of flowing blood. "I know him. Ozzie."

"What about Ozzie?"

"That was almost ten years back—when I modeled." Misconstruing Elaine Howell's tension at my elbow, she bristled. "You heard me, sister! I was in all the mags, even on covers!"

"This is Ozzie's wife," I said, bringing confusion to her tomato paste eyes.

"What's this, anyhow?"

"How'd you get on Ozzie's list?"

"For cryin' out loud, he played the field. Why pick me?"

"Ozzie picked you. Name and address on a list dated one month ago."

"So what? I'm known around. Maybe he heard I was here and wanted—" She glanced at Elaine Howell uneasily.

I asked: "Who collects your rent?"

"The Barker Corporation. What's that got to do—" An ivory phone interrupted her. I interrupted her move toward it.

"Answer it," I told Elaine Howell, then told Alice Smith, whose thin wrists fluttered agitatedly in my hands, "Take it easy. You won't be hurt."

"I don't like it," she whimpered.

I winked, spoke softly. "Relax. I'll square it with Nickie."

Her eyes widened. She whispered back, "For cryin' out loud, why didn't you say?"

I indicated Elaine Howell stooped over the receiver. The blonde's lips formed a scarlet O. She remained passive while I crossed the room and joined Elaine Howell's ear at the ivory receiver in time to hear a hoarse-voiced man say:

"—Not gettin' outta bed for anything this morning, Alice, baby. Know what I want you to do when you come over?" Without pause, he itemized his wants in graphic detail that warmed my cheek from the flush heating Elaine Howell's. When he concluded, "Can you fix me up in, say about an hour?" Elaine gasped:

"I can fix you up sooner than that! Go at once to a psychiatrist! You're sick! You're disgustingly, neurotically sick!"

And slammed the receiver into its cradle.

Then turned with me to face Nick Roachi entering the apartment behind his own key. After him came an elderly, bespectacled man and a young, overly muscled one, glowering. Alice Smith whimpered, "Nickie, they bust right in!"

"Lieutenant Burt," murmured Roachi, who looked the middle-aged saloonkeeper he represented himself to be and, in part, was.

"Police?" whispered the older man. When Roachi nodded, he stepped toward me, saying, "Officer, I presume you have a warrant for—" and found himself propelled by Roachi's arm back into the muscled glowerer.

"Blow," Roachi told him, then them: "Both of you."

The glowerer made a production of memorizing my features before following the other out. Roachi displayed large teeth. "Anythin' I should know, Pete?"

"Mrs. Howell," I said, motioning to Elaine.

He nodded, keeping his gaze on mine. "I made her from the news."

"She's checking Howell's affairs," I said. "They hadn't been married long enough for her to get the hang of them."

He slid his fedora back on his bartender-grey head. "What I don't get is your pitch."

"The Martin kill."

"I heard that's closed."

"It's been re-opened."

Carefully, he said, "Howell, I never met."

"Martin?"

"Well—" his gaze unsteadied, fell upon Alice Smith still portraying righteous indignation. "Standin' around like two bits! For cryin' out loud!"

"But, Nickie, they bust in on a call—"

"I have to tell you twice?" he shouted, reddening.

"Well, all right!" She hip-walked defensively to the bedroom. When its door slammed behind her, Roachi showed me his sweaty palms.

"I was down Miami the day Martin got it; that day, the day before and the day after. Me and him tended the same bar in the old days."

"How about lately?"

"Until I seen it in the News I didn't even know Howell was his partner, so help me!"

"But you kept in touch with Martin?"

His fedora bobbed toward Elaine Howell. "Pete, she thinkin' of takin' over?"

"She wants to know who's behind the Barker Corporation."

"Martin and me were pretty pally. You know?"

"You never told me."

He palmed his pink forehead, then showed me the palm and his large teeth. "Well, now you know."

The ivory phone began to ring. I asked, "Anything else?"

"So help me, Pete. You got it all."

I touched Elaine Howell's arm. "We can go now."

"But—"

"We got it all," I told her, urging her toward the door. As we reached it, Roachi spoke:

"Pete, you want I should settle?"

I faced him. He was straddle-legged on the ivory broadloom, sweating.

I told him, "Take it easy."

Walking down the corridor we could hear the ivory phone continue to ring unanswered.

A few blocks later, going West on 86th, she shuddered. "What a horrible life! Why do they do it?"

I shrugged. "I'd say Alice Smith prefers it to waiting tables. You didn't see the redhead in the bedroom who probably can't buy her heroine dreams any other way. The excitement lures some, others bounce into it from broken marriages. A few are forced. There'll be two or more in each remaining apartment on your husband's list. Add the weekly take and you're in very high finance."

"Don't jump to conclusions," she begged in a low voice.

"It's a step, not a jump, Mrs. Howell. One such apartment can buy the whole building in a few years. Then you have the Barker Corporation, a legitimate landlord whose books show only rent. The real net appears as 'profits' in the tax reports of Martin & Howell Investments. Not itemized. You won't find itemization—unless in the linings of your husband's other jackets."

She tugged fiercely at my arm, turning me to face her while pedestrian traffic eddied about us.

"What makes you so certain?"

"If you were listening, Roachi told us."

"He was so vague."

"His version of the Fifth Amendment."

"It's circumstantial."

"Most evidence is. On one hand is that character on the phone. He'd spend anywhere from two to five hundred for a few hours of Alice. On the other is your husband's two thousand plus notation. Probably a week's net, after overhead, which includes upkeep, rent and the percentages paid Roachi and the girls."

"Nobody knew my husband or Mr. Martin at the Barker Corporation."

"Try them with pictures. Or there may be one or more intermediary corporations."

"I can't accept it," she said, shaking her head. "I've known Oscar ever since I was a child. I can't just throw that overboard on the insinuations of such a—what is he, Roachi? A pimp?"

"Technically. I doubt if he still steers. But he provides bail and defense if the girls are arrested, protection, if they're bothered. Whatever they need. Probably supplies the redheaded addict."

She stared at me. "And pays bribes?"

"That, too," I nodded.

"He called you 'Pete'."

I watched suspicion flood her large eyes, and nodded slowly. "Like Alice Smith, I'm known around."

"He wanted to settle something with you," she breathed.

"He wanted me to forget the apartment."

"For money?"

"Probably."

Her voice was barely audible. "You would take that kind of money?"

"You take it!" erupted through my teeth. "Howell tried shielding you, to credit him that much—but you had to play with fire! Now you're burned, knowing you've been eating, drinking, dressing with exactly that kind of mon—"

I swallowed the rest, wishing I could retrieve it all.

She was rocking.

"Mrs. Howell, I didn't mean to—"

"Please!" she cut in painfully. "You did. You do. Assuming so much! I want those pictures. Oscar told me Mr. Martin was a business genius who was making us wealthy, which may be all Oscar knew of the business. Your conclusions point to Mr. Martin, whom Roachi knew, not to my husband, whom he'd never even met. And Alice Smith knew Oscar only as a playboy many years ago. You knew before we started that apartment held prostitutes, didn't you?"

I stared at her, proffering the packet of full-faces and profiles.

"But you kept silent," she went on, ignoring it. "Was it to shock me? Is that why you had me answer the phone? There's something frightening about you—as if you're trying to turn me against my husband. Are you?"

I could only stand there, frozen-faced, holding the packet toward her.

"You're so contemptuous of him," she breathed, finally taking it. "I felt that when I heard of your clever device to discredit his claim of having been struck down. But how could you turn me against him, Lieutenant Burt? However he may have violated the law, it was not after swearing an oath to support it. Who, accepting money from prostitution, is the worse offender?"

I stood there, shaking my head, groping for words that would not come. She twisted away, half running up 86th, until she was lost from view in the endless stream of pedestrians.

Remembering, as silvery bubbles began exploding in the little glass percolator cap, I felt as frustrated as I had then. 4:36 on my kitchen clock. Rain continued to beat softly on my kitchen window. My phone, and Elaine Howell in the living room, continued to be silent.

It no longer mattered who was the worse offender. That had been settled, once and for all, by Freud's demonology. But it had seemed to matter in the Police Commissioner's office, where Inspector Quinn's huge fist banged the Commissioner's desk:

"Now she's got the Administration doin' summersaults. What the hell's goin' on?"

"You want my badge?" I had asked.

The desk bounced. "I want facts!"

"It started with that girl on Fifth Avenue," I said.

"What girl?"

"Ten months ago. The sidewalk knocked her head into her neck. Cantelli."

Quinn stared at me. His growl softened. He turned to the Commissioner. "I sent Pete to find if she jumped or was pushed." He faced me again. "An eight floor drop, wasn't it?"

"Nine. A fur buyer from Detroit entertaining a Chicago buyer with two girls he'd rented for the night. The three survivors couldn't tell us much, but what they did stood up under the polygraph. The Cantelli girl had been on a crying jag, the last anybody noticed. I located the cabbie who'd steered them, and he led me to Roachi. Through Roachi, I learned she was broken up over missing a spot in a Broadway musical, and something about a romance she'd soured before turning pro."

The Police Commissioner cleared his throat. "That all of it, Lieutenant Burt?"

"All except, to milk Roachi, I had to act as if my hand was out. He still expects my bite. That's what Mrs. Howell caught. I'll repeat this under a polygraph, Commissioner."

"It won't be necessary," he smiled. "How did you close the case?"

"Suicide."

Quinn accompanied me from the office. "Vice has nothin' on Howell. Martin either, except that one rap eleven years back. The Smith broad was gone before we got there, and Roachi wriggled free on a habeas ten minutes after he was booked. That's one smooth organization. Who d'you think runs it now?"

"Roachi."

"Makes no difference," he growled. "The D.A. couldn't work it in unless Howell takes the stand, which he won't. She took it fightin', hey?"

I nodded.

"She stand a chance?"

"No."

"You better make sure, Pete. One little crack in your case, she'll squeeze him through. Mark my words."

∼

I marked the changes nine months had wrought in her when she sank into the chair facing my new desk, three days after the Court of Appeals refused any further postponement of Howell's execution.

Innocence, softness gone, her face could have been carved from pale marble. But she managed a faint smile. "Congratulations seem in order, Captain Burt."

Her smile faded when I replied, "I'm sorry they can't be mutual, Mrs. Howell."

"Not really, Captain. You despised—" She caught herself, nodded. "Of course. You're sorry for me, were from the outset, even in love with me. I felt that—why you tried turning me against Oscar, although I don't think you realized why. A subconscious—" She caught herself again, shook her head wryly. "If it will give you satisfaction, you were right about Oscar, about everything. An agency I hired found your intermediary, a Jackson Corporation which held all Barker stock. 'Jackson.' A euphemism for Jack Martin. And he was the obscure, solitary figure you said he was. But—" her eyes fastened on mine, "—you never once told me you believed Oscar shot Mr. Martin."

Five months after Howell's conviction, a case as dead as an old newspaper, as fresh to her as if Martin's cheek still bled. I said, "Believing or disbelieving is for the D.A.'s office."

"Yet you believed Oscar fattened on prostitution on much less evidence, a list of names, and Roachi's cryptic words."

I sought cryptic words to answer that, found nothing but the numbing impact of her stare.

She gestured tiredly. "I'm not trying to trap you, but there it is. More than anything else, your failure to accuse Oscar of shooting Martin helped me withstand all the disappointments. Alice Smith gone before I returned. All the other apartments vacated before the agency I hired could reach them.

Even Roachi. It took the agency a week to discover he was buried. Strangled in a doorway—"

I nodded. "Mugged. The case is still open."

"Open or shut, aside from Oscar and Mr. Martin, he was the only man I could associate with that filthy business. But it no longer matters. Last night I learned the man who shot Martin probably had nothing to do with the business."

"How'd you learn that?"

"Oscar finally talked to me. He'd feared my discovery of it would shock me into abandoning him. Strange," she murmured wistfully, "isn't it, Captain? I knew him a lifetime, was his wife a month, and met him for the first time last night."

"It happens."

"He equates prostitution to gambling, the laws against it unrealistic sops to prudery."

"Everyone rationalizes, Mrs. Howell. Those who don't— or can't take gas."

Her head shook impatiently. "I have no time for abstractions, explaining him, even weighing my attitude toward him. It changed, of course; but that can't affect my efforts to help. He's been deserted by everyone else, even his mother. The money is gone. Only my belief in his innocence remains. That, and one slight clue—"

"What clue?"

"The girl in the snapshot you took from his pocket when he was arrested. It was significant after all. He found it on the floor under him when he recovered consciousness. He pocketed it, fearing its implication. His main thought being to hide any trace of their business, he thought it belonged to Mr. Martin, the girl a prostitute. It wasn't until much later—a few weeks ago—that he realized Mr. Martin could not have dropped the picture."

"Why not?"

"It had not been on the floor when he entered the office. Staring down at Mr. Martin, he would have noticed it. And Mr. Martin, unconscious when Oscar was struck down from behind, dead when Oscar awoke, could hardly have put it there. Only the third man in the office could have dropped it."

I began to say, "Assuming there was—"

"There had to be a third man," she cut in impatiently. "After knocking Oscar down he stooped over him and fitted the gun in his hand to shoot Martin like that, with Oscar's finger on the trigger. He would have been too occupied to notice the snapshot dropping from his pocket, particularly since it slid under Oscar."

"How did he leave the office?"

"That porter lied. Or there was a way out nobody considered. I've had nightmares about it." She smiled faintly. "In one dream it was a man who could make himself invisible. I don't know how he left, Captain. What matters, he was in the office when Oscar entered, gone when Oscar awoke. The girl in the picture could have been a relative or sweetheart. The man could have traced, as I did, how control of the apartments passed through the Barker and Jackson Corporations to Martin and Howell Investments."

"Martin was shot with his own gun," I said.

"I don't think the man went there to kill him, but to thrash him. But Martin drew his gun, holding the man at bay while phoning Oscar to hurry over. And somehow, before Oscar arrived the man wrested the gun from Mr. Martin and struck him down with it, then struck down Oscar when he entered. Probably it was then he realized he could kill Mr. Martin and leave Oscar so compromised he would surely be convicted of murder. Is such a reconstruction ridiculous?"

Nothing about her was ridiculous. Done with Freudian demonology, she had used cold logic to jigsaw a snapshot and a handful of facts into a murder scenario that could need only some minor repairs and a breath of life to become true.

I said, "Overlooking how this fellow got out of the office, it holds together pretty well—assuming your husband's innocence."

"I do! Oh, he's rotten, guilty of preying on prostitutes. Anything despicable you accused him of, I would believe—but not that he shot Mr. Martin! I'm as certain of that as—as—"

"As you were of my honesty?"

"And still am!" she cried, her cheeks flaming. "From the very first moment I met you, I felt..."

Whatever she had felt lost itself in silence as two faces blazed across my desk.

She had difficulty digging the crumpled snapshot from her purse.

I had difficulty keeping my gaze on it. Still the dark-haired girl smiling into the camera from a ranch-house lawn, with the city skyline in the background.

She whispered, "How do I find her?"

"Rogue's gallery, if she has a record. If she hasn't—" I shrugged. "It would take a lot of time and money."

"I have neither. Only ten more days—"

I shook my head slowly, watching anguish possess her lovely face. Tears came to her eyes.

"There must be a faster way. I can tell the house is somewhere across the river—but there are thousands like that. The exact one wouldn't be necessary. A girl this pretty would be known over a wide neighborhood. Help me, Captain. Please—"

I shook my head again, my guts coiling into a knot.

A tear trickled down her cheek and into my guts and loosened the knot. Logic could not withstand demonology. Ask Freud.

I heard myself say, "Rent a Polaroid Land Camera. Have this snap remade in the size it takes, cross the river and move around. Keep taking pictures of the skyline. When you get one matching the original—same relationship among the buildings—you'll be getting close. Take along a micrometer. If one building is wider in yours than the original, you're too close, narrower, you're too far. When you get the closest match, show the original around in stores. Ring doorbells. Try the nearest precinct, post office—"

Long after she was gone, I sat staring at the closed door, memory of her smile warm in my eyes, her parting thanks sweet in my ears. Freud could have dedicated a chapter to me —if he already hadn't...

4:53 on my kitchen clock. On the window, rain continued to beat steadily, the skies weeping for Howell, for her, for me watching dark bubbles explode in the little glass cap atop my percolator. I considered pouring two cups, decided against it. Coffee murdered sleep, which I wanted above everything else. I took sleeping pills, and cold water to wash them down.

The news was still on her lap, Oscar J. Howell still glowering up at her. Her eyes tore away from the clock to guide her hands toward the coffee.

4:55. My phone continued silent. They were having a time locating Inspector Quinn. But they would. They always did.

I settled into the big chair facing hers and watched her face stoop to the steaming cup. When it was back on its saucer on the coffee table beside her, I said, "You found her."

"Her mother," she said. "Not her."

I said, "You were almost a year too late."

"Yes," she nodded. "Mrs. Cantelli still can't understand it.

Betty had been doing so well, rehearsing for a Broadway show."

"Mistaking hard boiled eggs for impending chickens." I said. "The story of her life. Actually, the closest to performing she ever came was hostess in a Spanish Harlem dance hall. Too ashamed to come home, having told everyone she was making the grade."

"Mrs. Cantelli said nothing about a dance hall."

"She doesn't know. I didn't—until too late, back-tracking from her suicide. One of those murky dives where the girls picked up extra money dancing hard against the Johns, personal grinds and bumps to a soggy climax. A step to Roachi and bigger money. The United Ballrooms, Inc., another subsidiary of the Jackson Corporation—"

"I knew it was something like that," she whispered. She glanced at the clock. I could no longer read it. The pills were taking hold. But I could see her face me again and hear: "Mrs. Cantelli thinks it was a broken romance. Betty told her she was engaged to a producer."

"He'd rented her for a week. It went to her head."

I could no longer meet her gaze, could barely see it. Sleep was tugging me deeper into the chair, thickening my eyelids, dulling my mind. Her voice seemed to come from a great distance: "Did you love her very much?"

"Ever since the Cantellis rescued me from the orphanage. Not her. My idea of her. I'd known her a lifetime, was engaged to her two years, and met her for the first time after she was dead."

"The way I met Oscar," she breathed.

"Except he won't die," I heard my own voice as from a distance.

"It's all in that report upside down on the table. When Quinn calls, tell him. Or get in touch with your lawyer, the

Commissioner, newspapers anyone. It's all spelled out. You'll get him back—"

Now the room had darkened, and the rain punishing my windows had become loud. Too loud. I could no longer speak over it, tell her how right she had been—

The snapshot slipping unnoticed from my inside jacket pocket when I stooped over Mama's Boy to fit the revolver into his palm and use his finger to extinguish Martin, that obscene whoremaster, who'd fainted when I slapped the revolver from his hand—

Only the souvenir baseball bat with which I'd struck down Mama's Boy threatening me—until I found the excuse to grip it and use it on my own head before it was dusted by fingerprint men—

Even her dream was true. Locking the door when that porter knocked, then hearing him wait outside, unable to leave. Hiding in the closet until the office bustled with investigatory activity, then backing out with the linen jacket. A homicide man among homicide men. As she had dreamed, a man who could make himself invisible, simply by being a cop among cops.

I began vibrating—almost back to full consciousness—found myself staring up at her strangely distorted face, her hands shaking me savagely. She was screaming:

"Those pills—did you swallow them all?"

Behind her the phone erupted violently.

"Quinn!" I yelled at her. "Answer it—"

"You fool!" she sobbed. "Oh, you fool—!"

Both of us, I wanted to say, but her face swam out of view. My lapels released, I sank back into the welcoming embrace of the chair. Freud's baby. Had it made, then chucked it away— so she could ruin her life being Mama Boy's substitute mama.

In the distance her voice was screaming: "I don't know how many! Too many! ...Ambulance... Please—"

And again, during an ebb in the tide of sleepiness engulfing me: "-to delay the execution further—because he fell in love with me. No, not a shred of new evidence, Inspector Quinn... Absolutely none... None... None—"

It took them four days to extricate me from the coma. No mention was ever made of my report. Inspector Quinn, who arrived just a few minutes after the ambulance removed me, found Elaine Howell sobbing near an ashtray piled high with crumpled ashes.

Six months later, he was best man at our wedding.

the big bust

"NAKED, she stood in the window, waving at me."

Albert Benson took another slow drag on his cigarette, brooding up at the grilled roof of his cell. In the adjoining cell two sobering drunks clung to the intervening bars, wide-eyed. A grin bared the yellowed fangs of the young deputy monitoring us through the door bars.

"Then what?" I prompted.

"She reached down to help me climb in the window. I thought she wanted—" His pale eyes sought mine. "You know?"

"What happened?"

"She wrapped her arms around me. Tight. I mean—" Cigarette smoke trailed his vague gesture. "Like warm and alive foam rubber. I got so hard I didn't know, try slipping out of my pants or just open my fly, you know? But before I could do anything she whispered against my cheek, 'Help me! I'm in trouble!' I whispered back, 'How?' She whispered. 'Behind you.' I turned to look—"

Benson took another slow drag. The tic was alive on the

left side of his face. A young, gaunt face. Almost haggard. I broke into his reverie.

"What then?"

He swallowed hard. "Then I woke up on the floor, looking at old Mr. Hobbs. Just as they were breaking in the door."

"With the poker in your hand?"

He nodded.

"But no naked woman," I scowled. "No woman. Just you, Hobbs in his easy chair and the poker in your fist, most of Hobbs' brains on the poker's business end."

"Like that," he nodded. "She'd gotten away somehow."

"How?"

"I don't know."

"They had to break in the door because it was bolted on the inside. The only other exit was the window—but the garden bed outside showed only one set of shoe prints, leading to the window. Yours."

"Mine," he acknowledged, the tic twitching his cheek with the regularity of a neon sign blinking on and off. "I don't know how she got away."

"You didn't dream her?"

"Dreaming women wasn't my problem at the hospital."

"What was?"

"That shell outside of Saigon. I'd keep hearing it come and watching the other grunts dive for cover. But I couldn't move. I just froze there until the whole world turned black, with flames licking through the black and hearing that awful silence. And then I'd wake up yelling. When it stopped happening they discharged me."

I said, "Five women on Hobbs' estate, according to what I'm told. Mrs. Eunice, the housekeeper, grey haired and dumpy. Vera, the maid, a skinny brunette. Helen Spain, Hobbs' secretary, also a brunette but, they tell me, stacked.

Mrs. Hobbs, a stacked blonde. And Madeleine, his daughter from his first marriage, a stacked redhead. Which was it?"

"I told you. Stacked. But I couldn't see the color of her hair. She wore a kerchief."

"How about under her arms? Between her legs?" Benson shook his head helplessly. I asked, "How about the color of her eyes?"

"She wore sunglasses."

"I thought she was naked."

"From her nose down."

"From her nose down, then. What distinguished her?"

He dragged heavily on the last inch of his butt, flipped it at the built-in commode, missed. I crushed it on the cement floor. He said, "Tits. They seemed to stick out a foot—and tilt up. Not Mrs. Eunice or Vera. I know them. They let me see Madeleine and Mrs. Hobbs and Helen Spain." He shrugged. "They were dressed."

"What did you expect?"

"Well, if they'd let me see their—"

"Fat chance," I said. "But even if they did and you picked one, it would be your word against hers and, considering the bolted door, who do you think a jury would believe?"

I singled the deputy to let me out.

Sheriff Lemuel Gainer drawled past the cigar stub in his mouth, "Always like to have a fancy private dick from the big city show us rubes our business. Ain't that right, Myron?"

The deputy bared his buttery tusks. "That's right, Lem. "

"Up hereabouts," the Sheriff went on, his overfed face featuring eyes the size and warmth of nailheads, "we're so simple, we figger a shell-shocked boy locked alone with a fresh corpse in a room nobody coulda left before we bust in the door sorta killed the dead man; 'ticulally since they'd been feudin' ever since the boy got turned loose from a GI psycho ward."

"Feuding about what?"

The cigar shifted from one side to the other of the slit trench he used for a mouth. "Tell him, Myron."

"Trespassin'," Myron said.

The sheriff nodded. "The boy's folks own four hundred acres right on the lakefront. But comin' back, addle-headed like he did, that didn't suit him. Wandered everywhere. Right through Hobbs' garden one time. Hobbs chased him with a hoe. Swore he'd have him committed back to a psycho ward. You know what Benson said? Tell him, Myron."

"A man who'd fence off any of the land God made for everybody wasn't fit to live," Myron quoted.

The cigar was plucked from the trench to jab at me. "And this from a boy whose own folks was just as rich as Hobbs, had just as much acreage fenced. You ought to know. They're payin' you."

"Their lawyer is paying me."

"How much?"

"About what you make in a year."

Myron's grin faded. The sheriff spat. A brass cuspidor a good ten feet from him rocked. He sleeved his trench, injected the cigar stub, said, "Can't blame the boy for his wild notion, how them wimmen run around up there. They follered us right into Hobbs' den after we bust down the door, clutterin' up our investigation. Tell him how they was dressed, Myron."

"Bathrobes."

The sheriff nodded emphatically. "Not a stitch under 'em, and pretty damn careless about lettin' us see tits an' pussy. Not Mrs. Eunice or Miss Vera. Local folk, with enough sense to dress decent. But that Missus Hobbs, an' his sassy daughter an' that high-assed secret'ry. Practically nekkid. Don't wonder the boy didn't imagine all three of 'em wavin' him into the winda. Hey, Myron?"

The yellowed teeth appeared up to their black roots.

"Who called you?" I asked.

"Mrs. Eunice. After she heard a loud ruckus in the den an' found the door bolted from the inside. It grew quiet when she knocked. So she sent Vera to phone us an' she stood right outside that door until we came. She'd been expectin' trouble right along, how everybody out there was allus tryin' to squeeze money outta old Hobbs. Right then he'd told her he was gonna take a nap an' not to disturb him. Prob'bly that's why he bolted the door in the first place. When we broke in young Benson was standin' over him kinda moanin'. The poker lay on the floor. We raised the nicest set of prints off the handle you ever saw. Benson's right hand."

"Can I see them?" I asked.

The cigar shifted. "Show him, Myron."

Myron produced a blow-up of the dusted poker handle and another of Albert Benson's right hand prints. The sheriff had not exaggerated. The impression was perfect.

"That's how it is, the Sheriff said. "The only thing that'll keep the jury from a guilty verdict five minutes after they leave the co'troom is they'll be laughin' too hard over that nekkid woman story to vote."

"If it gets to a jury," I said.

"Don't fret over that," he drawled. "The Gove'ment let him outta that psycho hospital, he's legally sane. No matter how many fancy shysters or fancy private dicks from New Yawk his folks waste their good money on, that boy is cooked. Hey, Myron?"

The yellowed dentures were dutifully unveiled. The brass cuspidor rocked. I wandered out in search of a phone.

～

"I go for the kid's story," I told Gilbert Harrison, one of New York's "fanciest lawyers," long distance.

"About the nude woman?"

"She was trapped in the den after killing Hobbs. Seeing Benson crossing the garden from the den's window, she slipped out of her dress and—"

"Why?" he cut in.

"To keep his attention off her face. She baited him in, slugged him, then planted the poker in his fist and vanished."

"How?"

"I've only been on the case a few hours, Mr. Harrison."

"And came to a singular conclusion," he said dryly. "On what do you base it?"

"Try swinging a poker hard enough to bash in a man's head and see if your prints won't smudge a little. According to those Sheriff Gainer has, Benson's didn't."

A thoughtful pause. Then: "That's a good point for the trial."

"If it comes to that. Have I a green light?"

"Yes. But—"

"What?"

"I understand popular feeling is against the wealthier element in that part of the state, and they'd be inclined to pre-judge the boy despite his fine war record. Be tactful."

I tactfully long distanced Joe Kenneth, Chief Investigator at Metropolis Underwriters, who reacted with characteristic warmth: "What the hell is it to you if we cover a Hobbs or a Benson?"

"One's up for scragging the other. I thought I might do you a good turn."

"How?"

"They're both loaded enough to be insured with a biggie like Metropolis, or one of your associate companies. On double indemnity, survivors will score big."

"Exactly which Hobbs and Benson?"

I gave him the particulars on both men, then listened to five minutes of long distance hum before Kenneth returned to pour oil in my troubled ear.

"You've got something, hotshot, and don't think I don't appreciate it. We're on the verge of paying Hobbs' heirs about six million. Benson's about half that. You got something?"

"I'm out to see Benson collects his old age pension."

"Fine. What can I do?"

"Have Hobbs autopsied."

"Why?"

"Hunch."

"Anything else?"

"Who collects on Hobbs?"

"Wife, daughter, a Miss Helen Spain, and about half a million spread among a batch of servants. On double indemnity, the wife and daughter get two million each, the secretary almost a million."

I said, "Hold the payments. Tell them it's under investigation and I'm your boy. I want a red carpet."

"How about my right eye?"

"Some other time, Joe. What I need now is a green light."

"And a red carpet," he sighed. After a pause: "Okay, hotshot, but—"

"What?"

"You've been known to cut corners. With Metropolis behind you, for crying out loud, take it easy!"

~

I settled easily into a brown Barcelona Chair while a sad-faced Mrs. Eunice, short and dumpy, as advertised, waddled away with my card. It floated back in long, slender fingers before the bulging jacket of a trim grey suit, below which cotton-clad calves tapered into grey suede shoes, and over which, over a ruffled white blouse loomed pale lips, a tight braid of jet black hair and horn-rimmed glasses.

"I have them," she said dryly when my gaze finally reached her glasses.

"What?"

"The usual female accessories. If your inventory is concluded, Mrs. Hobbs will see you in the writing room alongside the pool. I'm Helen Spain."

"Congratulations," I said, rising.

"For what?"

"Almost a million dollars," I said.

Her dark eyes were enormous behind glass. But expressionless. She said, "Follow me, please."

I followed her discreetly dancing rear accessories along a corridor and into a room full of sunlight, wicker furniture and a brace of frontal accessories that seemed a foot long and angled up.

They strained a blue silk Bikini within a carelessly draped white terry robe, below which issued long golden limbs. Above it I found myself being studied by a cocktail-lounge face topped by a cascade of hair so blonde it seemed white.

Helen Spain vanished as I mumbled amenities and settled in a wicker chair alongside Mrs. Hobbs. I became lost in her wide green eyes estimating my virility, fiscal status, and reaction to so unweedish a widow.

"It took us by surprise," she murmured in a husky brandy voice, fingering my card delicately. "What is there for Metropolis to investigate?"

"If Albert Benson's story is true," I said, "the woman who

murdered your husband wouldn't collect—according to State Law, which forbids anyone to profit from a crime. Her share would then be divided among the other heirs."

"But how could that poor boy's story be true?"

"That's what I'm here to learn," I said, unable to keep my gaze up. When I finally wrenched it back up, she was smiling.

"If you're going to suspect every large bosomed woman in this household—"

She broke off to gasp. Following her outraged gaze through the writing room's glass wall to the swimming pool beyond, I saw a pair of deeply tanned and very muscular arms pull from the water what seemed a stark naked girl of fantastic proportions. A second look enabled me to barely distinguish her flesh-hued Bikini.

Muscles, equipped with a black mustache to match his hair and very white teeth to set them off, yanked her up and into his chest. The shock must have been easily absorbed. Neither stepped back.

"Oh, that scheming little bitch!" breathed Mrs. Hobbs at my side.

Then only her robe was at my side, and she was through the glass door and swishing angrily across the flagstoned terrace toward the pair.

I lit a cigarette and enjoyed Muscle's confusion as he tried to disengage himself. The girl made as if to wrestle him into the water. Even from where I sat it was evident she only wanted to wrestle.

But the girl stepped back prettily when Mrs. Hobbs hove in view. The girl whipped off her pink bathing cap, exposing a head on fire. Madeleine, the redheaded daughter.

Glass and distance blocked their three-way colloquy. But not Helen Spain's breathless, "Was what you said true?"

She had floated soundlessly by my side.

"About what?" I asked, turning my hot eyes back to the tableau.

"That Metropolis is seriously considering Albert Benson's story?"

"True," I lied, watching Mrs. Hobbs slap away Muscle's placating hand.

"That hyper-sexed fool!" Helen Spain breathed.

I turned to stare at her, also staring out at the tableau, asked, "Who?"

"Rodney. He was Mr. Hobbs' chauffeur. Now—"

I kept staring at her. She was lost in contemptuous contemplation. I considered her flat heels, cotton hosiery, lack of make-up, horn-rims and braided hair. She antagonized me. I asked, "You against sex?"

"By itself, yes."

"What does that mean?"

"It needs a linked emotion—such as danger, fear."

Sudden realization of our topic swung her glasses around to me. An ironic smile curled her pale lips. "Don't get your dander up, little man. You inspire neither."

"Did Hobbs?"

Her smile faded. "He was sixty years old."

"But several million dollars young."

She frowned. "Are you investigating for Metropolis or Kinsey?"

"Yes. Why did he cut you in for half a million—almost a million now, at double indemnity."

"I was his secretary for twelve years."

"That's some bonus!"

"Mr. Hobbs was known for his generosity."

"You think Benson killed him?"

"Of course."

"How about the nude woman he saw?"

"*Thought* he saw," she corrected, shrugging. Her gaze

wandered back to the tableau—now almost upon us. Rodney's head swiveled between redhead and blonde as each bid for his ear. The pink and blue bikinis flanked his elbows.

Helen Spain spoke ironically. "Can you blame the boy for that particular hallucination—around this house?"

"Sheriff Gainer isn't the hallucinatory type," I said. "He saw you in a bathrobe during the confusion."

"And Madeleine. And Mrs. Hobbs."

"I'll ask them later."

"I'd been in the pool," she shrugged, then stiffened as the tableau erupted through the glass doorway and acquired sound.

"All I can say, Rod," Mrs. Hobbs was raging, "If you want to rob the cradle—"

"Cradle!" yelped Madeleine. She snorted. "You should talk! At least I'm not held together with Scotch tape and staples!" Before anyone could move, her hand made a lightning swipe, ending with a wisp of blue Bikini dangling from it.

Mrs. Hobbs' slower retaliatory swipe netted air. Madeleine had anticipated her. And now a wisp of pink Bikini dangled alongside the blue.

Leaving poor Rodney's and my eyes shuttling to and fro as at a championship ping pong match. I disqualified Mrs. Hobbs on the spot. She sagged. Madeleine stayed in the running, though, continuing out and slightly up.

The frozen spectacle was dissolved by Helen Spain's gasp. Mrs. Hobbs snatched up her white terry robe. Madeleine's triumphant smile slowly toured the reverent stares, ending with mine. She unveiled incredibly white teeth. "You're the Metropolis snoop, aren't you? Got a smoke?"

I tossed her my pack. She extracted one and lipped it. Her smile grew mocking. "I didn't think private eyes blushed."

"High blood pressure," I grinned.

"You're cute in a repulsive sort of way. What's your name?"

I struggled to recall what was on the card, then did. "Smith."

"As in 'John'?"

I nodded the lie.

"I still need a match," she said.

I considered personal delivery, wasn't certain I could surmount the obstacles. I tossed her a match folder. Rodney, better adjusted to these extraordinary fact of life, did the honors. Madeleine helped his hand bring the flame to her cigarette tip, stroking it. The flame jiggled.

Mrs. Hobbs was breathing heavily in the inner doorway, the terry robe tight about her exposed sags. Now I noted traces of veins amid the gold of her limbs, and that her hair and teeth were too white, her face too carefully done.

"Rodney!" she commanded.

Madeleine's fingers tightened on the match-holding hand. Smoke issued from her lips to extinguish the flame. She muttered, "Don't move!"

"Haven't you any shame?" demanded the older woman hoarsely.

Madeleine released Rodney's trembling paw and settled into a rattan armchair, crossing her flawless limbs. She murmured, "I have nothing to be ashamed about. Have I, Hawkshaw?"

She hadn't. Not a thing. But before I could wax rhapsodic, Mrs. Hobbs screamed: "I've had enough! Absolutely enough! Get out of my house!"

"Act your age," Madeleine snorted. "When Daddy's will is read it may be my house to throw people out of."

Mrs. Hobbs was toying with apoplexy. She turned boiling eyes on Helen Spain. "I will not have this place turned into a nudist colony. Have the pool drained instantly."

"Yes, Mrs. Hobbs," Helen Spain nodded stiffly.

"'Yes, Mrs. Hobbs,'" Madeleine mimicked. Then she drawled, "Listen, you stuffed shirt. I've had a bellyful of you for twelve whole years. I don't know what you had on Daddy to rate all that boodle, but it cuts no ice with me. That pool was just refilled yesterday, after being dry a month getting repairs. You let the water level drop one inch, you're fired!"

"Rodney!" screamed Mrs. Hobbs from the doorway.

Madeleine's cigarette made a commanding gesture. "Take one step in her direction, lover boy, you'll have to start from scratch again, chauffeuring rich old bags until you find another hot pants. Stay put."

Lover boy stayed put and waggled helpless brows at me. I waggled mine back at him, then said, "Ladies, if I'm permitted a question: How come you both appeared in robes when the Sheriff broke into Mr. Hobbs' den?"

"I'd been taking a nap," Madeleine shrugged.

Mrs. Hobbs, glaring at lover boy, said, "I was in the shower."

I looked at lover boy. He looked miserable.

"Rodney was taking a nap also," Madeleine drawled through a lazy smile. "Wasn't that coincidental?"

The slamming door heralded Mrs. Hobbs' departure.

Helen Spain spoke icily. "You have my resignation, Miss Hobbs." Her glasses swung to me. "Could you give me a lift to the station?"

"I'll be driving to New York in about ten minutes," I said.

She nodded briskly. "Ten minutes will be fine. My apartment is on the way—in Riverdale."

"There goes nothing," Madeleine scowled as the door closed silently behind the secretary. "For awhile, after mother died, she thought she was going to move in. When Daddy showed up married to Blondie she was in bed a week—

migraines." She snorted. "For that kind of migraine she should have fed aspirins to her bank account."

"I don't imagine you did nip-ups over the marriage," I said dryly.

"I could have killed him!" she frowned, then, noting my eager expression, smiled. "Could I have lured you into a window, Hawkshaw?"

"You have your points," I murmured.

Her laughter rattled the glass door. When it subsided, she said, "So do you, in a sort of off-beat way. Keep track of the society columns. If you don't see I've married lover boy in—say—a couple of months, look me up."

Rodney frowned. "Matheleine! Thith ithn't a pwoper thubject for dithcuthun!"

"Isn't he cute!" Madeleine squealed, grabbing his tan paw and yanking him down on her. The cigarette fell to one side, scattering sparks. Her fingers in his hair ground his face into hers. Her long limbs encircled his tan ones fiercely.

I got away from there. Minus my cigarettes—but smoking.

"It's preposterous to hold up payment," Helen Spain argued. She had appeared with two bags, thanked me for taking her, told me her Riverdale address and launched a battle for her near million as I tooled my Cutlass away from the Hobbs mansion.

Now, almost an hour later, her glasses glinting at the Taconic Parkway scenery skimming by, she persisted: "The boy evidently impressed you. But you can't shrug off a bolted door and his footprints in the garden."

"Sure I can," I said. "Berkley's door was bolted on the inside. It didn't mean a thing."

"Who?"

"Wall Street man. His study was bolted from the inside; the only window twelve floors over Fifth Avenue. When he didn't respond to the butler's knock, the butler peeked through the keyhole and saw Berkley sprawled on the floor. He summoned the building's maintenance staff to break the door down. Berkley's wife was with them when they did. She squeezed by them and flung herself on her husband, sobbing. By the time the police arrived they found that Berkley had died from too much hatpin in his heart.

Considering the locked door, they were about to write it off as a suicide. But one smart detective nosed around and learned Berkley was given to fainting spells. Got the wife on a polygraph and she broke down and confessed. She'd driven in the hatpin when she flung herself on him."

The glasses glinted at me. I watched the Taconic unravel before us. She asked, incredulously, "Are you suggesting someone entered with Sheriff Gainer, picked up the poker and killed Mr. Hobbs with it, unseen by the Sheriff?"

"Of course not. Just that bolted doors can be circumvented." I swung onto the Saw Mill Parkway and told her, "I guess a better example was the Watson Case."

"Another bolted door?"

I nodded. "In fact, the resemblance to this case is uncanny. A single pair of footprints crossing the snow covered lawn to the ground floor window of Watson's library. Inside, when they broke down the door, lay old man Watson, most of his head on a hatchet in the grip of the town drunk. Know what the drunk said?"

She sat motionless as I pulled up to the toll booth and parted with a quarter. We rode on in silence almost ten minutes before she asked, "What did he say?"

"You'll die laughing," I said. "He told the police he'd been walking along the sidewalk when this naked woman called softly to him from the library window. He told them he crossed the lawn and she helped him into the window—and the next thing she was hugging and kissing him and he got so excited, that's the last thing he recalled before waking up with the hatchet in his hand. Of course the police saw no naked woman in the library. And, again, this was a household full of women. You'd be amazed how one smart detective proved not only there had been a naked woman, but who she was. Watson's young housekeeper, who had anticipated becoming the second Mrs. Watson when the original passed away, having been sexing him on the side throughout that first marriage. But when he showed up with a brand new second wife—"

I broke off to swing off the Parkway and onto Riverdale Avenue, picked up the thread: "Watson's powers may have waned below the need for two bedmates, or the second wife put her foot down. Whatever, there was a confrontation in the library the housekeeper concluded by parting Watson's hair with the hatchet; a confrontation loud enough to startle a maid dusting furniture just outside the library door. When the maid knocked to ask if anything was wrong, then tried the door and found it bolted, then listened to silence, she yelled for someone to get help and remained parked right outside the door. The house-keeper-mistress realized she could not leave by either the door, where the maid would see her, or by the window, where the virgin snow would show her tracks. That was when she spotted the town drunk staggering along the sidewalk beyond the snow-covered lawn."

"Here," Helen Spain whispered.

I had already spotted the number on a blue canopy crossing the sidewalk. I waited for a grey Mercedes to move out, then backed into the slot, killed the ignition and turned to the glasses rigid on me.

"Go on!" she breathed.

"I tell you this dame was quick-witted?"

"Never mind the elaboration. Please go on—"

I shrugged. "She simply shed her clothes, wrapped a kerchief about her head to conceal her hair's color, put Watson's sun glasses over her eyes. Superfluous precautions. With what she displayed in that window, that poor souse wouldn't have noticed if she had three eyes and tusks. He went after what he saw, crossed the lawn, crawled into the library window, and—"

I broke off to glance at my watch.

"Go on!" she urged.

"Some other time," I said. "Didn't realize it was so late, Miss Spain. I have to eat, then check some things and—"

"What things?"

"Things."

She said, "Why not lunch in my apartment?" I stared at her. Her glasses were off, disclosing large eyes so deeply purple they were almost black; her pert nose flanked by cheeks tapering delicately to the tremor of her lips poised in an uneasy smile. She whispered, "It's not only that you've whetted my curiosity, but—"

"But what?" I found myself whispering back.

"Checking that boy's story," she went on unsteadily, "you had the opportunity to examine Mrs. Hobbs' breasts. And Madeleine's—"

"True," I breathed.

"But not mine."

I could have by-passed the elevator and floated her two bags up the eleven flights to her apartment. She had me leave them in the apartment's foyer, then led me into a large room where my popping eyes scarcely permitted me to hear her low-voiced, "Mr. Hobbs had it decorated. He liked to come here, as a sort of refuge from the family. What is your usual lunch?"

"Jack Daniels," I low-voiced back, my gaze glued to the innerspring rug on which a loud voice would have been blasphemous.

"The bar is over there—"

I wrenched my gaze up and discovered a low teakwood bar —but not Helen Spain.

I was not surprised. Lions crouching in the corner would not have surprised me. Nor a genie or two floating about. Nor a giant eunuch guarding the tapestried wall through which she must have vanished.

Eschewing Jack Daniels, I poured a shot of Pinch Bottle and mellowed it with tap water from the all-purpose bar, then bore the drink on a reverent tour. All four walls were tapestried, making of the room a desert oasis, each tapestry showing dunes of pale sand stretching endlessly into starlit darkness. About the fabulous rug were strewn low divans and hassocks, and low hung brass lamps cunningly illuminating all.

I ended on—or, rather, in—a royal purple divan, my shoes on the flaring buttocks of a laughing dusky wench twisting half-heartedly away from the clutching paws and enormous erection of an eager Nubian.

"Please go on about the Watson Case," urged Helen Spain's muffled voice from somewhere to my left.

My wandering gaze fell upon a laughing Arab joyfully impaling a fantastically proportioned houri to their obvious mutual enjoyment. Wherever my gaze wandered were variations of the same. An Arabian harem. Functioning.

It took effort to remember I was not there to browse in erotica. I took a sip of heather, picked the tapestry through which I thought she had vanished and said, "There wasn't much more, Miss Spain. When the naked housekeeper got the drunk to goggle at Watson's remains, she nudged him with the hatchet's blunt end. She wiped her prints off the hatchet's handle and snuggled it into the drunk's lax hand. Then she simply put on Watson's robe, bunching her stained dress under it, and hid."

"Where?"

I gazed transfixed at what transpired among three imaginative houri and the triple-chinned letcher in their midst.

"Where did she hide?"

"In the library closet, Miss Spain; probably hunkered deep among whatever Watson had hanging there, although such a precaution would have been unnecessary. When the cops broke in, finding corpse, weapon and red-handed suspect, they had no reason to search further. By the time the town drunk mumbled his story she had already emerged from the closet to stand around with other bath-robed women of that household. She would have gotten away with it, too, if a smart insurance detective hadn't found the one chink in her alibi."

"What was that?" Helen Spain whispered from somewhere in the room behind me. I had been addressing the wrong tapestry.

"Well," I arose on the buttocks still evading the Nubian's erection, as they had for years, possibly centuries. I shuddered and said, "Her excuse for standing around in a robe was she'd been swimming in the Watson pool—at a time, this detective later discovered, when the pool had been dry, undergoing repairs."

Her voice was unsteady behind me. "There was no Watson Case, was there?"

"That what I called it?" I murmured, turning. "Slip of the brain, Miss Spain. That's how I solved the Hobbs Case—"

My shoelaces almost popped.

Her tight braid had become a cascade of black silk flowing

to her ivory shoulders. All of her was ivory, undulating down to the harem. Tears glistened in her enormous eyes. She was trembling. I broke into a sweat.

"What will they do to me?" she asked hoarsely.

I shook my head. She swayed. I caught her. She clung to me, her face inside my shoulder. I whispered into the sweet-scented softness of her hair, "It's not that bad—"

"It's horrible!" she moaned. "Jail. Even worse—"

"Not without a case." I soothed, stroking the silky contour of her magnificent back, wondering wildly how I had ever thought Madeleine Hobbs qualified. Madeleine should have crawled into a hole and hid for shame! Helen Spain had my chest of fire. Albert Benson's description churned in my memory: like warm and alive foam rubber.

I murmured, "Even if Gainer figures it the way I did, which I doubt, it would still be Benson's word against yours. There's no physical proof that would stand up in court. And, at this late date, he probably couldn't make a positive identification even if they lined up all the Hobbs household bare breasts in a row, which they won't."

"He was going to marry me, just as you said," she whispered into my chest. "But when he brought her back from Palm Beach, he swore she'd tricked him into marrying her by getting him drunk. Swore he'd get rid of her and marry me as he'd promised."

"You found out he was lying?"

"In his den that morning. When I confronted him there and asked him how long he expected me to wait, he just sat there grinning at me. I bolted the door and picked up the poker and told him he couldn't play me for such a fool. He just kept looking at me with that mocking grin—"

"Easy, kid," I murmured as she began trembling in my arms.

"It was as if I wasn't doing it," she whispered hoarsely. "As if I was a spectator, watching the poker rise and slam down on him again and again and again." Her tear-smeared face turned up to me. "I'm so terribly, terribly frightened—"

"It'll work out I whispered almost into her lips—then closed the gap and tasted her tears on their tender softness. And lost more control as her hands slid up behind me and brought my head harder into hers so her lips could burn into mine. She wedged her hands between us to rip open my jacket. It fell behind me even as she yanked open my tie, looped it back over my head and tore open my shirt, unbuckled my belt, zipped open my trousers and pulled me closer toward her as my trousers crumpled to the rug and I stepped out of them. I took care of my shorts myself, considering the obstacle they had to surmount before dropping. What did it matter that she had launched the same process with young Benson—only to leave him earmarked for prison?

All that mattered was the electricity slowly knitting every frontal inch of me to every frontal inch of her in sparking flashes that killed all thought—everything but her sudden moan as we made the final connection sinking down to the fabulous rug. "Don't stop now! Damn you—don't stop!"

We entered the harem.

And entered it again the following night.

Sex by itself left her cold. But coupled with other emotions like a sense of danger, a sense of fear—she became a human passion bomb, explosively insatiable, utterly incredible, absolutely fantastic.

For an entire week of Arabian nights—until the evening my eager knock failed to open sesame her door. Instead there issued language that could have fissioned plutonium.

She had finally learned that young Albert Benson was once again trespassing at liberty, the Metropolis-instigated autopsy having disclosed that old Hobbs had died of a massive heart attack a good fifteen minutes before her raging poker began scattering his grey matter, accounting for his "mocking grin" which had driven her to such fury. And it was little more than a misdemeanor to bash in the head of a corpse.

I got Metropolis to release her single indemnity check the following morning.

She had earned it.

alas, mystery!

GENTLEMEN; although I recognize you lack patience to be led up by ways of exposition, demanding, in common with your generation, to be aped from introductory to conclusion as the crow flies, I am of another generation, in apable of stripping narrative of its flesh and serving only its bones.

Your importance is indisputable: District Attorney, Police Commissioner, and you others, personnel of this great city's Homicide Squad. And I appreciate your need to supply answers to the queries being among the reporters outside the door to this luxurious apartment. But I must proceed at my own pace.

Even now the wire services and networks must be spreading to the remotest corners of the earth each driblet of information as you gather and release it. His death alone would have been a headlined sensation. That he was slain and by a man almost half his size, almost twice his age, will, no doubt, purple journalistic prose for months to come.

I must, however, deny your charge of murder. It is true I plucked the tomahawk from the wall bracket where he kept it and drove it through his skull. If it astonishes you that one so old and enfeebled as I could have overcome such a large and powerful man, fury, gentlemen, was the equalizer. Yet "murder" is an inaccurate descriptive. I executed him.

It was undoubtedly presumptuous of me to usurp your function, and that of judge, jury, and executioner. But he had smiled, and that was at once his confession and death warrant.

You have seen that his was not a face readily capable of so gentle a grimace. His hawk features and the jet black of his hair and eyes italicized a somber expression. Add his intense stature, the dark ensemble he affected, and his swinging stride and you can visualize my shock this evening when, turning the corner at Carnegie Hall from opposite directions, we collided.

You cannot begin to imagine my terror when he gripped my arms with such ferocity I feared bones would snap. But when he uttered my name in recognition, terror gave way to shame.

Poverty is an estate impossible to disguise; nor can identity be readily concealed by the impoverished. This dropping grey mustache had enabled me to escape the notice of others I had once known, but not his. And, once recognized, my dreary history was immediately evident. As he saw, you see my rag-patched suit, fastened with twine in lieu of buttons; and there, Commissioner, on the floor behind your left foot, is the badge of my present calling: that cigar box with its display of shoelaces.

It had been a recurring nightmare that someone who knew me as I was would discover me as I had become. But even shame fled when his stern features struck a mnemonic chord and I recognized Gannett Blake's last improbable butler, Oswald Witherspoon.

The incongruous name surprises you, as it probably would the millions of his devotees even now learning of his extinction. But so cloistered has been my life that I knew him by no other. Nor did he correct me when I met his proffered hand and returned his greeting: "My dear Witherspoon!"

Certainly he was, in his fashion, a splendid host. In those dishes remain crumbs of such a meal as I had not savored in a decade. Afterward, sipping wine, he sat in the chair you occupy, Mr. District Attorney. I sat here; and between us, as you see, was the fireplace.

Now embers are fading into grey ash, but *then* ruddy flames licked hungrily at a cedar log, and its sap crackled in the meditative silence that fell upon us. Silence, as you know, is inherent in his breed; mine was for lack of a topic with this man I barely knew.

Whatever his thoughts, mine sped back through the years to Gannett Blake's first mention of him. If my verbatim quotations evoke skepticism, let me state here that I am cursed by that murderer of sleep, total recall. Of Witherspoon, Gannett had stated: "If he isn't the Last of the Mohicans, I'll eat him raw, my ulcers notwithstanding. I challenge his claim to another tribe. Whence came 'Oswald' or 'Witherspoon' confounds my imagination. But I tell you that 'fabulous' is too paltry an adjective. Oswald can mount stairs on his hands, eat glass, drive needles through his cheek, swallow fire, straighten horseshoes with his bare hands, accomplish practically anything you ever witnessed at a carnival sideshow. I lured him from one. And his wife is shyness incarnate. The merest attention sends her scampering like a startled fawn; a two hundred pound fawn, I might add. A weekend at Miasma in their proximity would provide material for your next five books. This week, old man?"

It was an invitation I could ill afford to spurn. My livelihood, in those days, rested precariously on his good graces. I went prepared to face humiliation as well, as did the four other guests at Miasma that weekend. It was true Gannett's promotion finally overcame the snobbery which had withheld our work from the more genteel bookshelves of America, but that role did not suffice him. It was his custom to bring we five together where he could prod our natural jealousies into the open and, when the vitriol was at full tide, intervene in the guise of a benign mediator, in effect reassuring himself anew of his dominance in the field of detective literature.

I see your eyes explore the bookshelves in this room. You will not find us. Here is space only for hardcover editions of monstrosities calling themselves "mysteries," wherein the only mysteries are how many women will be violated, how many characters beaten or butchered.

With the possible exception of Hilary King, our names will be familiar only to the oldsters among you: Earl Fields, Dell Bagger, Agnes Chester, and, with due modesty, Rudolph Xerxes. Modesty notwithstanding, we five had established the ground rules, so to speak, of the detective novel. A Mystery then had been urbane, intricately fashioned, subtly evoking cerebral suspense that was relieved, at the climax, by a deductive strike. Settings had color, characters style, and, of utmost importance, the moral tone was high. Readers were confronted by intellectual challenges, not outrages to their sensibilities.

I concede that among authors of that era appeared Hammett. But while our followers flourished, his were properly relegated to the equivalent of today's comic books, the dime pulps, taken seriously by few. Nor would they be regarded seriously today, these literary degenerates, these apostles of sex and sadism, was it not for the macabre murder of Gannett Blake that fearful weekend.

If the Commissioner will permit me, I am aware of the so-called facts you cite. No, I was unaware you are related to Gannett Blake through marriage. But I assure you the news reports and family belief that Gannett Blake died of smallpox are false as well as immaterial. There are, as has been said, "wheels within wheels." If I may be allowed to proceed without further interruption.

I thank you, sirs. With due respect for your relationship, I must state that Gannett Blake, that Saturday at Miasma, gave a performance too vile to even be called characteristic.

This was at a time when his hypochondria had seized upon the then novel fad of allergies. On this Saturday, cats were anathema, and one he had surprised in his bedroom had thrown him, so he claimed, into a horrendous sneezing fit.

His temper remained brittle. Clara Witherspoon, a massive woman with a rather pretty face, was repeatedly sent into stammering flight by his pointed comments. He drove Oswald Witherspoon through his assorted paces, goading him into straightening a horseshoe, climbing the porch steps on his hands, biting, then chewing and swallowing a chunk from a glass tumbler, driving needles through his cheek, and demonstrating his fire-swallowing technique. And although Witherspoon performed with stoical nonchalance, I suffered embarrassment for him, and learned, through muttered asides, my resentment was not exclusive.

Our turn came that afternoon as we were gathered in Gannett's den awaiting the refreshment he called "High Ten." Even now I wince at the memory of his turning to me and demanding, "What takes you so long, Rudolph? Ten pages of dissertation on gland extracts before a setting is laid or a character introduced! Is it any wonder Havermill reviewed Door Sinister as he did?"

Havermill, that frustrated author turned critic, long since in his miserable grave, but then venting poisonous spite on his betters. I scorned the review. Earl Fields had the execrable taste to quote it: "Creaky."

A novel, gentlemen, that took eight months of painful labor, and then went on to sell in three editions. Creaky! Oh, I had a petard on which to hoist Fields! Knowing Gannett's sadistic object, yet unable to restrain myself, I cited Chandler's devastating review of Fields' Scream!: "Eek!"

Rather clever, eh? Unkind, perhaps, but justified. Absolutely justified, I assure you.

Without quoting further, the session, as was usual, degenerated into a deluge of brickbats from which not even the sedate Agnes Chester was exempt. Indeed, with Gannett showing no inclination to mediate, as had been his wont, we actually may have come to blows had not Oswald Witherspoon entered to provide a diversion. In his laconic style he announced, "That cop's here about shootin' Miss Dunby's cat, boss."

To this day I remain ignorant of "Miss Dunby," "the cat," and "shooting," for no sooner had Witherspoon been dispatched to conduct the "cop" thither than Gannett unfolded his slender six feet and stood looming among us, all pretense of humor gone. He addressed us thusly:

"Miss Chester and gentlemen—" And I cannot reproduce the utter nausea in his tone as he ejaculated the last, "—Blake House verges on bankruptcy. Why? Your cutie-pie detectives! On the stage, the screen, in novels—all around us—people are going in for solid chunks of raw life. They leaf through a Blake House novel and what, pray tell, do they find? Peter Pan twittering around a Maypole in pursuit of a Halloween mask! Instead of Life, parlor games! Sliding panels! Screams! Gland extracts! Murder contrivances out of Rube Goldberg! Dialogue that died with Henry James!"

Wagging a stern finger whose admonition included all, he bade us: "Listen carefully. About to enter is an officer of the law. Watch Sheriff Banner in action. Rube he may be, but he meets in life what your assorted pansies will have to learn to meet in fiction if you're going to go on being published by Blake Hou—"

The remainder of his thought drowned in a gargantuan

sneeze. Another followed it, bending him half over. His incredulous gaze drew ours to the small procession emerging from beneath the settee on which he had been lounging: a coal black cat followed by four tiny kittens. Tails aloft, they crossed the den and arrived at the door just as Oswald Witherspoon opened it to admit a stocky man in an olive drab uniform.

Sheriff Banner, I correctly assumed, although introductions were never performed, for Gannett's sneezing continued with mounting violence, almost tottering him from his feet.

It is immaterial which of us first sprang to his aid. In short order we were all, we five authors and Witherspoon, gathered about him, contributing to his support. I recall Agnes Chester demanding that a doctor be summoned—and then that she screamed.

Whenever a subway express rounds a sharp curve and its wheels shriek protest against the rails, it was a sound like that. I remember gaping at her. She was drawing back from our tight circle, staring down at her hands. I had the absurd impression she wore rubber gloves, then I became aware of a liquid warmth crawling along my own hands, drew them back, and saw it was blood.

Blood, gentlemen, stained all our recoiling hands!

Gannett stood swaying in the center of our widening circle. Then, with a sigh I distinctly remember, but which he could not possibly have uttered, he sank to the floor and rolled slowly to his back, arms out-flung, leaving us the awful view of his throat slit almost from ear to ear.

You look incredulous, Commissioner. "Smallpox," the newspapers proclaimed. "Smallpox," your wife's family believed. And, indeed, "smallpox" will forever remain the official cause of his death. For though a baker's dozen of us knew the truth, it can no longer be proven, the whereof I am approaching, if you will, but curb your impatience.

Your incredulity now is pale contrasted to that experienced

by at least five of the six of us gaping down at the corpse that was Gannett Blake. Agnes, Dell, Hilary, Earl, Witherspoon, and myself had all recoiled from Gannett almost simultaneously. All continued to stand with reddened hands out-thrust. And, before any of us could move, Sheriff Banner took command from the doorway. He had drawn the revolver from the holster at his side. Holding us under menace of the weapon, he bade us remain motionless, then made his way to the phone on Gannett's desk and summoned aid.

Clara Witherspoon appeared in the doorway behind a high-wheeled cart bearing the viands which were to have been our "high tea." Her reaction to the sight of her employer on the floor was to whirl and flee, screaming. The released cart, retaining its momentum, rolled forward—until halted by Gannett's out-thrust foot.

"Which one of you did it?" demanded Sheriff Banner, his call completed, fixing pale, narrowed eyes upon each of us in turn.

Six tongues remained silent. It was incredible, fantastic. As though frozen in our postures of recoil, six pairs of blood-stained hands remained visible—with no trace of a weapon in any of them.

Sheriff Banner muttered, "I'll be damned!" correctly summarizing our common status. He ordered, "Stay put until the fellas come and we're through searching you," then reached past Dell Bagger and appropriated a deviled egg sandwich from the cart.

In a state of shock, the human animal eschews thought for blind instinct, and often for instincts seemingly unrelated to the cause of shock, as Jung and Freud have so deviously explained. Nero fiddled. Men on the gallows have jigged and sung. Excess of sorrow laughs, Blake wrote. How else explain why all six of us automatically followed the sheriff's example.

Not until my third or fourth bite into the ham sandwich I

had chosen did awareness of my reddened hands register. And then, as automatically as they had been taken, the other partially consumed sandwiches followed mine back to the cart.

Agnes Chester gaped incredulously at her hands. I could tell by his quizzical expression, Hilary was storing for future use this revelatory glimpse of our essential animalism. Oswald Witherspoon regarded somberly the remains of the cheese sandwich he had almost entirely consumed. Dell and Earl stared at one another in horror.

I found myself pondering whether our instinctive atavism rooted in infancy, when the panacea for all sorrow is the nipple. I know that is a psychological explanation for obesity; the fat individual seeking the remembered relief of eating for his tensions. A provocative question, it still beguiles me. Then my concentration on it may well have been another means of escaping the unbearable reality confronting my eyes. But this is a morass I could explore endlessly, and I see by your fidgeting that you lack patience to explore it with me.

Only Sheriff Banner seemed unaffected. He retained control of the situation, denying Earl permission to stoop to Agnes Chester's assistance when she crumpled silently to the floor. Nor would he permit us to speak, even to summon Clara Witherspoon with a washbowl and towels to cleanse the stains from our hands.

He held us motionless until his aides arrived; three deputies, a doctor who served as coroner, and a large woman he addressed as "Hilda." All of whom, it will interest the Commissioner, were related to Sheriff Banner.

I wish to emphasize the thoroughness of his procedure. One at a time we were taken to a bedroom and stripped bare. Our clothing was examined minutely, our persons probed in shocking detail; Agnes Chester's by the woman, Hilda. When this search failed to disclose the weapon, attention was directed to Gannett's den. No paper was left unturned, no book unrifled. Inch by inch that room was searched, including the food cart and its cargo, and even the remains of our sandwiches. Subsequently, I learned that not only had Gannett's corpse been subject to the same procedure we had undergone, but it had been dissected as well, on the fantastic hypothesis the murderer may have disposed of the fatal blade by stabbing it completely into him.

Sheriff Banner even went so far as to fashion a crude blade of ice of the dimensions the coroner determined the murderer's blade had been. But the test model was necessarily of such thinness it failed to even puncture the skin of his wrist before shattering.

Mind you, gentlemen, six of us had been actually touching Gannett at that dread moment—one gripping a blade no thicker than an ordinary knife blade, but of the size, the coroner determined, to inflict a three-inch thrust, half an inch wide—yet no trace of it could be found!

By the following morning, after a sleepless, all-night session in which each of us, in turn, was subject to intensive interrogation, only the blade's likely identity had been established: a glass letter opener now missing from Gannett's desk.

Sheriff Banner, if the Commissioner will pay me close heed, was most delicately situated. If he charged any one of us with murder, the same evidence would apply equally to the other five. If he arraigned all six of us on a charge of homicidal conspiracy, the evidence would be overwhelmingly in his disfavor. It had been to our financial interest that Gannett remain alive, no matter our personal attitudes toward him. And this applied as well to the Witherspoons, now facing unemployment. Along with this was the extreme unlikelihood five mutely antagonistic authors and a brace of servants they barely knew would unite in such a heinous venture.

On the other hand, Sheriff Banner faced a difficult struggle for re-election the coming November. His failure to secure a conviction for a murder committed before his very eyes could destroy him politically. Nor did he alone face the prospect of a shattered career. Imagine the wave of laughter that would sweep America should it be learned the five foremost authors of detective novels had been unable to unravel the method whereby a murder weapon had been made to disappear from their very midst.

The "wheels within wheels," Commissioner. I will not here disclose who originated the suggestion that was finally adopted. Suffice that "smallpox" was entered by the coroner on Gannett's death certificate, and that, for the purported safety of the community, Gannett's remains were promptly cremated. In postscript, let me add that all citizens of that county were compelled to submit to vaccination, a display of official vigilance that helped return Sheriff Banner to office that Fall.

Silence, of course, was to the self-interest of both parties, literary and political, and sworn to by the third, the Witherspoons, and that same Sunday we all abandoned Miasma for our various destinies.

Perhaps it was inevitable the matter could not end there. I will not strain your patience by itemizing the various suspicions that came to me in the ensuing months—Agnes Chester's familiarity with occult japery, for example, or Earl's renown with sleight of hand, Hilary's adeptness with darts, Witherspoon's various talents, Dell's penchant for writing of illusive weapons, particularly those fashioned of ice. Nor will I detail here how I came to learn that each, in turn, considered me suspect. That phase passed quickly. There being no official "murder," such speculation could be no more than academic. What continued to obsess us was the disappearance of the letter opener. No reader of detective fiction, securing in his knowledge of the puzzle, no matter how baffling, be solved at the climax, could begin to appreciate how insidiously this actual mystery gnawed at our minds.

It was understandable that we perpetrated what reviewers came to call "coincidence." There can still be found on library shelves Fields' *Vanished Blade, Stab!* By Bagger, Agnes Chester's *Invisible Dagger,* Hilary King's *The Opened Throat* —and my own *Thrust Sinister.*

Less pardonable were our subsequent works, few of which reached print. As a case in point, my *Sinister Snee* was flatly rejected by Singlenight as "old hat." It met an equally dreary reception in every other publishing house of repute. The public, they claimed, was satiated with disappearing weapons, no matter how cunning the method or starling the solution.

Regardless, the problem obsessed me. How could a blade vanish before the eyes of five amateur criminologists and an officer of the law? Any other plot I contrived seemed so pallid by comparison that my typewriter kept disgorging half-filled sheets of copy paper until I again bore down on this haunting issue.

That the others were similarly obsessed grew evident as the months flew by and no more of their titles reached print. Only Hilary found an escape, establishing the mystery magazine that bears his name; but even in it, during its first years, I noted an abundance of tales involving the mysterious disappearance of murder weapons. But, in ensuing years, even Hilary bowed to the trend.

For the reading public, alas, retained its voracious appetite. And unto the breech opened by our collective inability to abandon this obsessive problem plunged the followers of Hammett. As such, gentlemen, as taste breeds art, art breeds taste. Fed by raw sadism, spiced pungently with sex, the reading public's taste changed. By this time, we five escaped our common obsession long enough to contrive other plots the reading public, so agents and publishers informed us, no longer deemed palatable. And then the American Detective Story, as millions had grown to know and love it, passed silently from the scene.

Of my sorry descent to the estate in which you find me, I will not dwell. Only shall I note how full realization that an era had ended smote me the day following my encounter with Dell Bagger in an elevator descending from Happer's offices, each bearing a rejected script. We strolled down Park Avenue in silence a while, and then Dell sighed and said, "Mine is an artificial hand with a blade concealed in the finger."

"Mine," I told him sadly, "is a hairpin made of tempered steel, filed down to a cutting edge, and returned to the woman's hair prior to the search."

"Agnes married Earl," he said.

"I know," I said.

"They opened a grocery in the Bronx," he said.

"I know," I said.

"Hilary is good for a touch about once every four months," he said.

"Thank you. I will keep that in mind," I said.

We parted, and the following day I read of his leap from a window of Big, Black. That was the day an exasperated editor of Quicksilver Mysteries told me, "Get off this puzzle jag, Xerxes. Readers no longer want to think; they want to feel. Have you read Scallone's latest? Trapped by this gorgeous lesbian who had murdered the only woman he ever really loved, her knife swaying in his back, he sweet-talks her to her knees on the floor beside him, murmurs poetically of his dying love for her, brushes her lips with his, kisses her neck, her throat—and bites through her jugular!"

I fled, retching, resolved never again to type word to paper. A resolution, gentlemen, I have never forsworn.

And still the question kept returning to haunt me, and its seeming insolubility evoked the sigh this evening which caused

Oswald Witherspoon to break our mutual reverie by inquiring, "You feel all right, Mr. Xerxes?"

"I was thinking of that terrible weekend," I informed him.

"Turned out okay," he shrugged. "Blake was no damn
good."

"I know," I nodded.

He scowled. "All that freak stuff. Like I was a dog showin'
off tricks. I didn't mind for me. Clara, though. That's the day
I found out what he'd been doin' to her."

I studied his impassive face in the fireglow, thinking here
was a subject I had neglected: Witherspoon's complacence to
Gannett's outrageous requests had seemed so equitable. I
asked, "What had he been doing to her?"

"Cussin'," he muttered darkly. "I found her in the kitchen
before the fireworks. Cryin'. Came out he'd been cussin' her
right along, just to make her jump. She was kind of—"

"Sensitive?" I supplied.

He nodded. "Yeah. And that mornin' he found her kitty
in his bedroom. The one you saw, only it hadn't had kittens
yet. Woke him up sneezin' and he yelled for Clara to take it
down and drown it. Her kitty. She like to died. And then,
when she bent over to get it, he pinched her. I was so damn
mad—"

"Did you confront him?" I asked.

He shrugged. "Didn't get a chance in all that mix up."

"All that mix up," I sighed.

He asked, "How about you, Mr. Xerxes? I never expected
a fine gent like you to wind up peddlin'. Don't you still write
detective stories?"

"Not the modern kind," I told him sadly.

"What stops you?" he queried. "The hard stuff?"

I nodded.

"Suppose," he said, leaning toward me earnestly, "you tied
in with someone who digs it. I mean, you know all the fancy

trimmin's. It could pay you a hundred, maybe two hundred a week—just sayin' where it should level soft where it should jump hot. See what I mean?"

"No," I confessed, meeting his intense stare, baffled, and at the same time disturbed—hopefully, I hasten to add, for a hundred weekly dollars, not to mention two, was an income I had long ceased to envisage even in dreams.

He asked, "How do you think I rate all this?" And his gesture encompassed the luxury of this apartment.

"I considered it in poor taste to actually inquire, although," I admitted, "it does provoke my curiosity."

"I started as a model," he said. "Fella who used to visit Blake. After the mix up he looked me up to model for his artists—ran an outfit called Grisly Comics. Paid me seventy a week. After a while I caught the hang of that stuff and gave 'em a couple ideas. I mean, you thumb out a guy's eye, I know how it looks. Then one of his writers said why give myself away? Tell him the ideas, he'd work 'em into a book and we'd split fifty-fifty. After the third book, the publisher, Karf, said, 'Where does this monkey rate half? I could hire pencil pushers at a flat rate and pocket the difference.' So that's what I did and it caught on. Radio. TV. Movies. And the books. Now I got three writers workin' my ideas into stories, only they got no class. Everybody gives me lumps: preachers, newspapers, schools—they're all ridin' me. So I figure if a high-class writer like you gives these three clucks the office how to finesse it; well, it's better'n peddlin' laces, isn't it?"

I quote verbatim, gentlemen, but it mostly struck my ears as gibberish. For clarification, I asked, "You mean you employ these writers to weave your ideas into acceptable literary form?"

"That's it, Mr. Xerxes," he nodded. "Only they don't know how to spit it fancy."

"What sort of ideas are involved?" I asked.

He gave a shrug. "Well, one of the best wound up in my fifth book. Sold two million in all editions. This guy's stabbed in the back by a dame readyin' to give the shiv a last nudge. Stallin' for time, he softens her up with love talk and gets her close. She falls for it and lets him kiss her and keeps kissing her, and when he gets to her throat he bites right through it. That even got wrote up in Winschell."

His face brightened at whatever he saw in mine. "You read it, huh, Mr. Xerxes? I'll bet you never thought Oswald Witherspoon was Mickey Scallone, huh?"

To tell you I was stunned, gentlemen, would be gross understatement. I well understand the knowledge Oswald Witherspoon was actually Mickey Scallone comes as no surprise to you, and is, indeed, why his death merits such imposing attention. But conceive my reaction! If ever there was a personification of the disaster which overtook my beloved *métier* and myself it was he, Scallone, the pace-setter of literary degeneracy, bellwether of the cesspool fiction which has elbowed its betters of America's bookshelves!

No, no, no, no! It was not for this I slew him. My reaction was one of shock, not rage. In fact, it turned to one of irony— that Gannett's death should fulcrum the seesaw which elevated Scallone by the descent of Xerxes!

Had Gannett actually died of smallpox, our output would have remained unaffected. Mystery's citadel would have remained impregnable to this sewage which inundated our literature, our culture, our very civilization. Yes, our civilization! Is it so far-fetched to ascribe the horror that stalks this city's streets at night to the public's warped reading taste?

Smile at one another if you will. Your thoughts are transparent: that this interrogation would be more fittingly concluded in Bellevue. But you all know the fable of a horse in battle losing a shoe for want of a nail, and how for want of a shoe the horse was lost, which led to the loss of a skirmish, which led to the loss of a battle, and then a war, and finally, a kingdom—all for the want of a horseshoe nail! Is it preposterous to conclude that for want of a solution to the mystery of Gannett Blake's death a genre was lost? And for want of that a culture was poisoned? And because of that a generation of children was nourished on Grisly Comics, went on to Mickey Scallone and then emerged on our streets with such values as "love is rape," manliness is sadism, and quickly acquired wealth the highest goal in life? Look at your precinct blotters!

Witherspoon did not wittingly launch this process. Nor did I pluck his tomahawk from the wall and drive it through is skull for being Scallone. I, as much as anyone else, allowed him the opportunity to become Scallone. He succeeded because five otherwise excellent minds failed to penetrate an enigma that, in the final analysis, was so ridiculously simple, the thought of it now sickens me.

As a matter of fact, the generosity of his offer moved me deeply. Instead of excoriating him, as you may have supposed, I gave him thanks and begged his leave to consider the matter. The issue tabled, we drifted once again into silence.

You can readily imagine the maelstrom of thought in which I was engulfed. At its core, inevitably, whirled the enigma with which my fate had become so inextricably entwined. And so it was, seconds before I was provoked to seize the tomahawk, my frustration burst through my lips in a passionate disclaimer: "I would sell my soul to learn how that letter opener was made to vanish!"

He nodded soberly. "That was tricky, all right."

"Tricky?" I protested. "It was diabolical! Take Fields—an amateur magician, but sleight-of-hand, under those close circumstances, was impossible! Enamored of the occult as Agnes Chester was, could she have brought us all under a hypnotic spell? Inconceivable! Sheriff Banner disposed of Earl

Bagger's pet literary device, the ice dagger. And the letter opener would have been found where flipped, no mater Hilary King's vaunted skill at darts. I was innocent as a newly born babe. And Garnett, had his hypochondria induced him to believe his own death imminent, hardly could have contrived such grisly self-destruction, even as a final gibe at us. Leaving you, my dear Witherspoon. And, with no slight intended, old man, I scarcely think you capable of conceiving and executing a method as subtle as this one must have necessarily been. Certainly you could not have stabbed the letter opener into yourself, as you did needles. And it was highly implausible that, as with the bite from that glass tumbler, you inserted it in your cheese sandwich, chewed, and swallowed—"

He smiled then.

And I understood at last.

ape

1

Her voice was strained: "Can you drive?"

I stooped to bring my eyes level with her horn-rimmed glasses. Behind them, her face was encircled by a dark green scarf. A dark green raincoat billowed down from her neck.

"I can drive," I said.

"Please," she said, moving over on the seat to give me room behind the wheel. "Wet roads make me nervous."

One for Ripley, I thought. Wet roads made her nervous; but two hundred and eighty pounds of hitchhiker rising six and a half feet to a flat-nosed face didn't?

I walked around the front of the big car and glanced back at the patrol car that had brought me to Midville's city line. No reaction from it. I squeezed in behind the wheel, switched on the ignition, released the hand brake, shifted into drive and started us toward the long hill east of Midville. In the rear vision mirror I watched the patrol car start its U-turn back toward the city prison. Behind us Midville began to shrink and tilt into a huddle of rooftops and spires.

Among them my former Cadillac, my former twenty-three thousand dollar bankroll, thirty days of my life, and eleven suspended months of imprisonment waiting to be unsuspended should I ever have the misfortune to be found in Midville again.

Never! I swore silently, lowering my gaze from the mirror. Ahead, through tiny raindrops smoothed into fan-shaped sheets of wetness by the flicking wipers, the road snaked up through green pastures punctuated by occasional huddles of cows and patches of tall corn.

"Tom Larson," I said finally, remembering my manners.

She murmured, "Norma Gardner."

"Well, hello."

Silence.

I said, "It doesn't really matter where I wind up, although New York would be nice."

"Please!" she moaned. "Please watch the road!"

Her business. Mine was the road. It reached a crest, wound along about a mile of drizzle-soaked countryside, then began descending. We came to a brake-screeching halt just short of a cross-roads. The radiator dipped salute to the raised palm of a state trooper.

Behind him, the intersection was blocked by a patrol car. Others flanked the road. Rain-coated troopers eyed us from both sides.

Watching the trooper approach, I murmured, "You hot, honey?"

The knuckles of her fists answered me. They were screaming white, pressed into her stomach as if it ached.

That was all I needed!

The trooper had a young, sullen face that broke into a tight grin when he stooped to look at me.

"The Ape himself!"

"Mister Larson to you, sonny!"

His grin widened. "Hey, guy! You rate a grouch after a month with those Midville Keystones. Why hit me with it?"

"Why, indeed?" I rejoined, feeling my stomach relax.

"That dame really have a needle?"

"My bottom is still pin-cushioned."

"So you dumped Angel Murphy on her. What made you pick on the referee?"

"He was climbing up my back and yelling he'd have me barred from every ring in the country. All I did was pick him off my back."

"And dump him on Angel Murphy trying to crawl back into the ring."

"Murphy crawled back in."

"You chucked him out again."

"Just to convince him the first time was no fluke. He'd gotten to believe the publicity handouts."

"So half the arena tried gettin' at you and you kept chuckin' 'em out—until the riot squad landed. I hear they fined and sued you down to your pants."

"Just about," I shrugged. "They settled for all but what I'm wearing and a hundred for get-out-of-town money. What's going on here?"

The trooper's gaze flicked past me, yawned at the girl, returned. "Bank job. Two of 'em got as far as the sidewalk. They're in the morgue now. But not until they'd killed a cop and a teller. The other three got away with two hundred and twenty grand. We—" He broke off as a station wagon braked to a halt behind us. "Okay, Ape—I mean, Mr. Larson, *Suh*! Two of the guys were described, and together they wouldn't add up to you."

"Why couldn't I be the third?"

"On account she was the sort of dish made the cop's

shoelaces pop open just smiling at him. He told that much before he died."

He stepped back and waved us on. We nosed around the patrol car, speeded up to fifty-five as we once more skimmed through the drizzle-soaked landscape.

The girl was slumped now, her head back against the headrest, her eyes behind the hornrims closed, her long-fingered hands in her lap now, as relaxed as her profile.

I could almost smell Midville's jail again. Helping a moll through a roadblock. A relaxed moll now. Calm, long-fingered hands, her nails scarlet, as if they had been dipped in blood.

A cop's blood?

Not for me! I touched the foot brake until the big car slowed enough, then wrenched the wheel and brought us to a pair of ruts winding deep into a stand of tall pines. The rear wheels skidded and jumped as mud fountained behind us. When only trees filled the rear-vision mirror, I jammed the foot brake and we slued to a halt.

Our hands met at the glove compartment as hers was emerging with a silvery revolver.

No contest. I closed my hand over hers, peeled her fingers away, and lifted the gun free before she could blink.

She huddled as far back as the seat allowed, staring at her revolver now practically lost in my fist. It sickened me. Guns, knives, blackjacks—weapons of any sort sickened me. I squeezed both fists on the gun and its barrel became a silvery U. I cranked open the window and tossed it into the drizzle.

She was staring at me, breathing hard. Traffic noises slithered mutely back and forth a good distance behind us. We were isolated in a world of dripping trees.

I said, "Let's do this once more. I'm Tom Larson, ex-wrestler, ex-practically everything, bound as far away from Midville as I can get."

Her tinted glasses remained motionless on me. I reached

over and plucked them free. Enormous violet eyes sprang to view. I plucked off the dark green scarf, revealing a sunburst of coppery hair. I pointed to her dark green raincoat.

"Do you take that off or do I?"

She said, "I have about two hundred dollars in my purse."

I said, "Add two hundred thousand and nineteen thousand and another eight hundred and we'll be in the ballpark."

She stopped breathing.

I pointed to her raincoat. Her scarlet-tipped fingers trembled on the clasp beneath her chin. They trembled down the row of clasps. The raincoat opened wide—and there she sat in a cream-colored turtleneck over a cream-colored skirt that flared down from an extraordinarily slender waist over full hips to tanned, sleek calves.

My shoelaces did not exactly pop open. But she was not smiling.

"What that Trooper mentioned," I said. "You the girl from that bank job?"

Her head turned slowly from side to side.

I said, "Don't misunderstand this. I just have to make certain—" And I put my hands on her.

I had to disengage one to intercept her clawing nails. I had to force a thigh over her thighs to imprison her thrashing legs. Terror whimpered from her lips as my free hand moved slowly over her; down each curving side, up her front, down her back, then all the way up inside her thighs.

Along the way the message got through—that my object was search, not rape. And she quieted, letting my hand discover that there was nothing under her cream-colored outfit but panties and a bra and herself.

2

Herself was almost too much. Quashing my instincts, I

reached past her to unlatch her door, returned her scarf and raincoat from where they had landed at her feet, then nudged her out into the drizzle.

Two hundred and twenty thousand dollars, probably in hundreds, would make a fairly bulky package, I figured. But then again, it could have been scattered about in small lots. So I looked under the floor mats, as well as under and behind the seats. The dash compartment held only a flashlight and a cream-colored purse. In the latter, along with two hundred and sixteen dollars and change, was a California driver's license made out to Norma Gardner, with a Santa Cruz address and a photograph that was grounds for a libel suit. There was a car ownership registration made out to one Jack Colby, with a Columbus, Ohio, address.

Further evidence of a man turned up inside the brown cowhide suitcase on the rear seat where, amid lingerie, I found half a dozen BVD briefs, size thirty-four, and over a dozen pairs of navy colored nylon stretch socks.

I pocketed the car keys and stepped into the wet, unable to determine whether the wet streaming down her cheeks where she stood on the other side of the car was tears or drizzle. I told her she could get back inside, then went around to the trunk compartment.

Here, one of a matched pair of airplane luggage held a man's wardrobe: a grey suit, a navy suit, cream-colored slacks and turtleneck, several white, grey and pale blue shirts, a batch of assorted neckties, scuffed carpet slippers, two pair of black oxfords, more navy colored stretch socks and assorted underthings, the other female stuff. The tool kit held nothing but tools. The spare tire was pumped full.

I encircled the full perimeter of the car, feeling under the fenders, then raised the hood and spent five minutes finding nothing but its greasy self.

Looking in the open window at the driver's side, I discovered it had not been drizzle but tears streaming down her lovely cheeks. "Where's Jack Colby?" was all I could think to say.

"Dead," she whispered. "He was run over by a milk truck."

I ran out of things to say.

She went on. "Last week. We were supposed to be married this afternoon."

I stared at the drops streaming down her cheek.

She stared at the drops streaming down the windshield.

I wished Angel Murphy was on hand to throw me away from there. I wished I was back in the Midville jail, I wished to be anywhere but where I was. I tossed the car keys into her lap and turned to wade back through the muddied ruts toward the highway.

She caught me halfway there, stumbled after me through the muck to grab my arm from behind, bringing my ape face around. "Please don't leave me here! I couldn't drive—couldn't do anything! Help me—please!"

"After I shoved you around like that?"

"Yes!" she cried, raising tremendous violet eyes for me to drown in. "I needed shoving around. Like slapping someone to stop hysterics. I've been in a daze all week. You're so big—strong—self-confident. I need that so much!"

That was her need. Mine? After a month in that stinking jail, after practically a lifetime of frustrations—I felt stunned just staring down into those pleading eyes, feeling myself sinking into them.

"Please!" she begged again, misunderstanding my silence. "I feel so—lost—"

Both of us. Beauty and the Beast in the wilderness. Lost—

Her long fingers tugged at my wet sleeve and we slogged back to the car. I helped her in, went around the front and came in the driver's door, met by a tremulous, tear-streaked smile. If my shoelaces popped, I could not tell. I was lost.

Her hand caught mine inserting the ignition key. "I'm Norma Gardner," she said. "Ex-fiancee. Ex-practically everything. New York, Tom?"

"It doesn't really matter," I shrugged. "I'll be starting from scratch. Where isn't important—as long as it isn't Midville."

"I'm starting from scratch also. All I have is that two hundred dollars and Jack's car. I took it and drove. Just to be moving. He had nobody. Neither have I."

"What'll you do now?"

"I don't know."

"You and me both."

Her eyes seemed to be trying to swallow mine. "Won't they let you wrestle anymore?"

"Oh, you heard that trooper—?"

"I was there with Jack the night you threw that other wrestler onto that woman at ringside."

"They were trying to shove me into a cage."

"I don't understand."

"My face. My size."

Her head shook slightly. "I still don't understand."

"That hag stuck me with a darning needle whenever I got in range. And she kept yelling, 'Send that ugly ape back to the zoo, Angel Boy!' And when the point in our script arrived when Angel Murphy was supposed to drop me with his so-called 'Heavenly Spin,' he laughed, 'Here you go back to the zoo, you ugly ape!' so I dropped him on her instead."

"How can people be so awful!" she said. Releasing my hand, she added: "Let's go, Tom. Any direction you want. But keep talking. Keep talking. Make me think of anything but myself."

3

Later, I had no distinct memory of getting back to the highway and continuing east. I had a vague memory of the big car skimming past farms and through small hamlets in the rolling countryside, of stopping once for gas and once for a quick lunch at a roadside diner, and of the drizzle giving way to bright sunshine from an almost blue-black sky decorated by occasional shreds of white fluff.

Mainly, I recalled talking—all the way back to the orphanage, and then the Larson farm that became my foster home because I was the biggest and strongest kid in my age group at the orphanage, and how the local authorities forced the reluctant Larsons to release me for schooling, and how I always had to struggle with the powers in the various schools who wanted me for their teams when I would have rather softened my macho image by cultural pursuits, but how my athletic prowess ultimately effected my release from the farm by affording me a football scholarship to a fairly decent Midwestern University, and how there the dichotomy persisted—all the pressures on me to perform versus my pursuit of some career having nothing to do with my size or strength—and that I finally had to settle for a degree in business administration.

I did not, of course, go into my psychic development, particularly how Norma Gardner seemed to be the materialization of the only up-beat dream I ever had. The one recurring again and again through the years—where I met a beautiful girl who needed my help, a girl who looked past my mashed nose, my outsize jaw, my lumped brows and all the other scars of battle my face and size had forced me into. A girl who looked past the ape mask to the inside me, the guy who wanted to live a decent, normal life, loving and loved.

And she seemed to be thawing in her own way. Her tears vanished. Color seeped back into her cheeks. Even with the tinted horn-rims hiding her gorgeous eyes again, the dark green scarf again concealing her magnificent hair, the dark green raincoat again shrouding her incredible form, she seemed to me more beautiful than any of the sirens who had peopled my dreams through the years.

Over dinner in the booth of a roadside restaurant, it was as if a phantom named Jack Colby never existed. Just the two of us discovering each other over food I later could not recall ordering or tasting.

The mood cracked a little when she said, "But Tom, everybody has—I mean you must have had some girl friends."

"Thrill seekers," I shrugged. "The only ones coming on to me wanted me to drag them by the hair into a dark cave."

"Surely, you exaggerate!"

"Look at me!" I told her. "Take off the blinkers and really look! Try to imagine yourself married to me!"

The crack in my euphoria widened a bit when she actually looked—and got the expression, the one all non-thrill seekers eventually got, the one that stirred the snake to movement deep in my gut. Which influence my expression—because a flicker of alarm entered hers.

Her hand crossed the table to grip my wrist. "Hey, Tom! Let's not make a federal case of it, huh?"

I forced a grin. "That's the score, Norma."

"Give yourself a chance to grow on me, for crying out loud!"

And the crack closed.

Half an hour later, riding into gathering darkness, she said, "We'll have to stop pretty soon, Tom."

"Motel?"

"I'm going to say something. But no federal case, huh?"

"Say it."

"Separate rooms."

"Of course," I said, but felt a hot tide flood my face nevertheless.

~

They were not completely separate at that. They were joined by a common bathroom with outside as well as inside latches on the doors, so either party could insure privacy.

I had not gotten to the point of locking the latch on her door when the poster caught my eye. From the Thurston City Bowl—fourth stop of the wrestling tour after Midville. A yellow poster alongside my image in the washstand mirror. Like seeing my face twice.

In the poster version, the artist had lowered my hairline, narrowed my eyes, thickened my nose, fanged my teeth and matted my torso with coarse black hair. All I lacked was a club and a Neanderthal cave in the background. The artist had been kinder to Murphy, putting a deep wave in his peroxide blond hair, whitening his teeth, shadowing a dimple alongside his smile and suggesting a halo over his head.

ANGEL MURPHY vs. APE LARSON

I ripped the poster from the wall, shredded it and deposited the shreds in the wastebasket under the sink, then stripped to my shorts and soaped my practically hairless torso.

Rinsing myself, then blotting the wet with a fairly thick white towel, I studied my face in the mirror. Thirty days in the Midville jail had not altered it a whit. Only one small strip of tape on my forehead remained as a memento of the Midville riot squad's nightsticks.

My face, my erstwhile fortune. Any cartoonist's idea of a thug. Hollywood's stock image of the rapist who drags the heroine off into the bushes. Promoter Bill Ferguson's potential nationwide TV villain—until Midville violated his sacred wallet, rupturing our umbilical cord forever.

My face, my cross. I had never in my entire life really

grown accustomed to it. Now, drying it, my nape tingled and I looked around to find Norma watching me from inside the door I had neglected to latch.

Her lips were parted slightly, her eyes almost round, as if in wonderment, as they slowly traveled up my musculature. They lingered on my pectorals, even as mine dwelled upon what hers did to a filmy black robe.

Pink faced, she whispered, "You through, Tom?"

I nodded.

"You're quite a hunk of man!"

"If they had your face, we'd make terrific babies."

Both our faces caught fire.

She whispered, "Goodnight now."

I stood outside my bathroom door until I heard her throw the latch from its other side, then crawled into the double bed and lay back remembering the feel of her under my exploring hand, and gradually drifted off to my usual nightmares—

Like the first and only time I ever played post-office, with the seven boys holding odd numbers, the seven girls even. The first girl called, "One," the first boy, "Two." By the third time around, with "Thirteen," my number, yet to be called, I began to catch on. Eleven years old, I began to learn who I was. Confirmed when, from a group of giggling girls, one voice rose loudly enough for me to hear: "Don't ask me! I don't want to be kissed by a gorilla!"

I walked blindly out of there, and kept walking most of the night, getting back to the farm after the 5 am milking, and getting a licking for missing my chore. But I did not care.

I knew, at last, who I was.

Like the occasion I crashed through their line in the Cotton Bowl in time to block a punt with my chest, momentum carrying me past the kicker. And I caught the ball coming down behind him. Forty empty yards to their goal line. Almost thirty of them gone by the time the chant from the stands penetrated my consciousness:

Ape! Ape! Ape! Ape! Ape! Ape—!

My knees melted. My fingers turned to butter. The field came up and slapped my face as the other team landed on my back. One of them picked up my fumble and ran ninety yards to a touchdown. A game that ended seven to nothing.

I knew who I was.

As did employment managers who fingered my magna cum laude business administration diploma and all my professorial recommendations and, considering the effect of my appearance on their customers and office girls, said, "Sorry, Mr. Larson."

As did girls I wanted whose eyes protested they had no wish to be kissed by a gorilla—or girls I did not want who had difficulty keeping their thrill-hungry hands off me, pleading to be ravished by a gorilla.

Send that ugly ape back to the zoo, Angel Boy!

Even in dreams, I knew who I was.

And, of course, my solitary up-beat dream—now acquiring clearer definition. Now her hair was a coppery sunburst, her eyes liquid violet, her lips poised in a gentle smile, her low voice rising in a fierce scream.

Scream?

"Tom! Help me!"

I jerked awake staring at the shadowy ceiling, memory of the scream fading, as happens with dreams.

I lay there not breathing, straining my ears. And then I heard a man's low, insistent voice—and something else. Sounded like bedsprings?

My feet hit the cool carpet. I sat there, knuckling my eyes, straining to hear more. No question about it. Not dream stuff. A man's urgent voice accompanied by irregular sounds of what could have been bedsprings. Through the two closed bathroom doors.

I became aware of another sound, a radio turned to a newscast, something about the fright of a morgue attendant when a "corpse" named Anderson sat up and spoke to him.

It sounded louder when I entered the bathroom, as did the man's voice whose words were now distinguishable: "Talk to us, you goddam bitch!"

I crossed the bathroom on bare feet and put my hand on the other door's knob and took a deep breath as all the muscles in my body tensed. I did not know whether it was locked on the other side. It would not have mattered. A padlock would not have mattered. The door cracked open like a cannon shot, freezing the tableau beyond.

There were two men in the room with her.

The man with the cigarette lighter had to release her ankles, which he had been gripping with one arm while applying flame to the soles of Norma's bare feet with his free hand. He had to release the lighter, which dropped to the carpet alongside his knees and flicked out. He had to release Norma's ankles, which began kicking at his back with no perceptible effect. He had to yank a snap-blade knife from his jacket side pocket and rise to his feet as the blade flicked out.

By then my hand was on his knife-holding hand. I could feel bones splinter. I had a brief glimpse of the shock wetting his dark eyes as my other hand gripped his crotch and raised him over my head.

A dark-eyed, dark-haired man in a grey suit. About six feet. About a hundred and ninety pounds. The dark eyes had screamed at me when the blade dropped to the carpet from the lump of meat that used to be his right hand.

Split second impressions before I launched him—

The second man was shorter, wider. A balding, grey-haired man with a bulldog face and a bulldog build in a brown suit.

His problem was more complicated. First he had to release Norma's head. He had been sitting on her pillow, holding her red head tight against his chest by using his left forearm as a gag against her mouth. His right hand gripped her wrist in a hammerlock between them.

He had to release her completely. He had to try to get an automatic pistol from his shoulder holster as Norma whirled around to claw at him. He managed to jerk free of her and get the automatic out—just as his partner crashed into him.

I was a step behind.

I reached into the tangle of their bodies for the automatic pistol, got it, saw the bulldog head come up and raked it with the pistol's muzzle. Blood spurted from the balding grey head to the dark face.

I spun the pistol away and introduced both heads to my fists—again and again, stooping down to punch them, feeling the snake in my gut slithering, slithering.

Only vaguely did I become aware of Norma clinging to me, yanking at me.

She had slept raw, as I slept raw. She was tugging at my left arm and begging: "No more, Tom! That's enough! Stop it before you kill them—please!"

The two men were huddled motionless on the carpet. I stooped to feel wrists. Both had strong pulses. Both seemed a long way from consciousness. I straightened up, growing more and more aware of Norma's magnificent breasts flanking my left bicep. I said, "Okay. The cops can have them now."

"No!" rushed out of her.

I caught a quick case of goose pimples.

"No cops?"

She pushed her face into my shoulder, whispered, "I can't explain now. We haven't time. You'll have to trust me." Her eyes climbed to meet mine, pleading. "Please, Tom. Trust me! We have to get away from here—immediately!"

I did not want to get away. I did not even want to cross the room and turn off the radio, now telling how Tony Martin left his heart in San Francisco. I wanted to keep standing there with her pressed against me. And more. I wanted to taste her lips.

They were soft, moist, clinging, with a faint salty taste of tears.

Her hands crawled up behind my neck as she brought herself directly before me, into me. My arms crossed at the small of her back and tightened, raising her off the carpet. Her tongue came alive against mine, probing, dancing. All of her against me seemed to become alive—then froze.

Her coppery hair flew back to show me the flux of emotions in her huge eyes. "Not here!" she breathed. "Not now, darling—"

It took more strength than I thought I had, but I managed to release her. She almost crumpled to the floor. I caught her, eased her to the disordered bedsheets. "Oh, Tom, they'd just started. I didn't think—"

I examined the slight burn under the arch of her left foot, then headed for the bathroom, turning off the radio en route. In the bathroom I found an almost empty jar of Vaseline, which I brought back and applied to the burn.

"I think you'll have to help me dress," she whispered.

I did, and by the time she was tightening the side zipper on her cream-colored skirt, both our faces were on fire. I turned away to examine the men on the carpet. They remained comatose. To insure it, I fetched the automatic pistol, removed its clip and yanked the slide to eject the last cartridge, then used its butt behind their ears. Their pulses remained strong. I looked up to find Norma's face still on fire. Eve, when the apple told her Adam was naked.

My own cheeks burning in the bathroom mirror were Adam's, when the apple told him he was naked before Eve. I washed the blood off my hands and arms before continuing to my room to dress.

She limped in with her suitcase as I was slipping into my jacket.

"I was afraid I wouldn't be able to walk," she said breathlessly, "but I can. It isn't so bad."

"Leaving them here is bad," I said.

"No, Tom. Anything else would be worse. Believe me!"

"I'd like to. But—"

"Not now!" she cut in urgently. "After we're safely away, please, Tom!"

I flicked off the light, swept her and her bag into my arms and carried her out to the car. All the other cabins in the motel were dark and silent. Nobody seemed to be around to mark our departure.

4

She murmured, "Why are we stopping, Tom?"

Her head was resting on my shoulder, her two hands encircling my right bicep. For two hours we had ridden in silence like that, swinging north at the first crossroad to get off the highway running past the motel—in case there was pursuit—then, about fifteen miles later, turning west to baffle pursuit even further. Now the sun had come up from behind to chase the night toward California, and I had swung the big car onto a pair of ruts winding into a stand of pines, much as I had the day before, albeit without the rage that had prompted me then.

"We'll get to why no cops later," I told the red sunburst on my shoulder. "Let's start with what those lads wanted to burn out of you."

"Diamonds," she whispered.

"Diamonds!"

"There weren't any. He didn't bring any back this time. I'd made him promise. But they'd followed us to Midville. Him, actually. He told me he'd given them the slip in New Orleans. Then, when they read in the Midville paper how he'd been killed, they began following me, thinking I had them."

"What diamonds?" I scowled incredulously down into her hair.

"I told you there weren't any. Oh, the other times—sure. Jack brought them in from Mexico, Canada, Europe. He was very good at it. Goff and Sinclair had jeweler clients for them all over America, and everybody profited. But not this time. This time he went to Mexico to let his suppliers there know Goff and Sinclair would contact them directly, Once we were safely away, he was going to let Goff and Sinclair know who those suppliers were. But he was killed before he could. I didn't know who they were. But they wouldn't believe me."

That made three disbelievers: Goff, Sinclair and my goose pimples.

She stirred as I reached past her for the flashlight in the glove compartment.

"What are you doing, Tom?"

"Looking for diamonds. Or two hundred and twenty thousand dollars. Or whatever else those two animals were torturing you for—"

"Suppose you found something?" She drew back and regarded me solemnly.

It stopped me. "I don't know, Norma. Yesterday, I'd have chucked you to the state troopers."

"To prove you didn't belong in a cage?"

"Something like that. I pay my taxes, cross at the green, take off my hat in elevators, never talk with food in my mouth.

Demonstrating that I don't belong in a cage is a good way to explain me."

"And now? If you find diamonds or money now?"

"Make it easy for me," I brooded down into her open lovely face.

"Tell me where to look."

A gentle, almost tender, smile softened her lips. "Everywhere—so you'll finally be certain. Start with me again. I promise not to fight you this time. All right, Tom?"

My hands found her again. It nearly tore me in half to finally pull them away and nod her out of the car while I intensified my search of the interior. This time I examined every square inch of the seat cushions and inner upholstery, seeking any trace of a slit into which something could have been slipped. I canvassed that car's interior inch by inch—and found nothing.

I got out, nodded her back in and went through the trunk compartment again, this time examining the luggage and everything inside for secret compartments. I felt my way through every garment, even checked the heels of Jack Colby's shoes. I unhitched the spare tire, swung it out of the car, then probed its nest and every inch of the trunk's interior.

I put the spare back in, closed the trunk, then got under the car on my back and, with the flashlight, examined every square inch of its underside. After that, I raised the hood and this time removed the air filter, disassembled the carburetor housing, probed the water inlet in case a waterproof packet had been suspended within it—all of which added up to more nothing.

When I got back in behind the wheel, Norma was slumped low in her seat, her eyes closed. I touched her shoulder. "Okay, Norma. No diamonds. No money. For now, let's play it your way."

No response. I shook her shoulder. She remained slumped. Her pulse was steady, strong.

I stared about wildly, seeking a house, but beyond the pines I could see only rolling fields. As I punched the engine to life she sat up and turned to frown up at me.

"Morning sickness, I think it's called, although I never passed out before. I'm supposed to have a craving for pickles and ice cream, but I don't. All I want is breakfast." Correctly interpreting my expression, she explained, "I'm going to have a baby, Tom."

Not diamonds. Not bank loot. A baby?

"I'm all messed up!" she sighed.

I said, "We can both use breakfast."

She reached past me to turn off the ignition. "First let's talk, Tom. Goff and Sinclair made me think of it. I'd forgotten all about the motel."

Now a motel? "What motel?" I breathed.

"About three months back, when he went to Mexico, Jack sent me to this town of Hampton. It's in the next state, about three or four hundred miles north and west of here. The motel's about ten miles the other side of Hampton. A nice old man—Mr. Hobson—was selling it at a loss because he wanted to retire to Arizona. It has a two-story house built over a gas station, and twenty back-to-back cabins, making forty in all. He needed two hundred and fifty thousand dollars. Jack said it was worth much more. I left a fifty thousand dollar deposit in Jack's name. The balance was to be paid out of income over twenty years, at thirteen and a half percent. Mr. Hobson never saw Jack, has no idea what he looks like."

She gripped my bicep with both hands, looking up at me intently.

"Go ahead," I barely breathed, as she paused.

"I told him I was Mrs. Colby. You said you graduated in

business administration, right? I was a darn good secretary for a real estate agency in Santa Cruz. We're both being born again, having to start from scratch. And, Tom, I can't do what so many unmarried girls do when they're caught. I want the baby!"

"Because it's Colby's?"

"Because it's mine! Because women are supposed to have babies! I don't want to be pushed into a cage either, Tom!"

I felt a hammer pounding in my chest, almost mesmerized by the intensity of her stare. I could barely utter: "So?"

"We're practically strangers," she went on. "But in another way we've become, well, close. Jack was no fool about money things. And if he said that motel was a fantastic buy, it was. What I'm thinking: after the baby comes, in return for giving it legitimacy, you can have half of what the motel will be worth by then. If we've gotten to like each other well enough to stay married by that time, no problem. If not, we'll get a quiet divorce, split what the motel is worth, and go our separate ways."

I could not speak. My throat was a knot. Sweat beaded all of me. Her nails dug into my bicep.

"Tom, last night you asked me to look at you and imagine myself married to you. I'm doing better than that right now. I'm looking at you and asking you to marry me!"

I was unable to squeeze a word past my throat. I could not say yes, couldn't say no—could scarcely think. I felt lost in a hot and cold fog, sweating like a pig, fluttering inside like a leaf in an Autumn gale. I punched the engine to life, eased the big car back to the highway, turned west again and brought the needle up to fifty-five.

"Those animals," I finally managed to croak. "Goff and Sinclair. They know about this motel?"

"Absolutely not. Jack intended to make a complete break with his past."

"Anyone else who might come after his leavings? Friends? Relatives?"

"Nobody. Like you, he was an orphan." She stirred at my side. I felt her eyes on me. Mine clung to the road. "Absolutely nobody, Tom. And people in Hampton never saw him. Not even his signature. He was in Mexico then. I paid the deposit with money he'd given me, opened a ten thousand dollar checking account in the First National Bank of Hampton and signed every paper as Mrs. Jack Colby."

Half a dozen miles raced under our wheels before I could choke out the next question: "When do you expect the baby?"

"About six-seven months," she breathed.

The suburbs of Thurston City gathered about us. I slowed to their thirty-five mile limit, parked in a diagonal slot before the Thurston City Arms and walked her into its coffee shop.

A nag-faced waitress dropped menus before us. I asked her, "What does it take to get married around here?"

"Rocks in the head!" she snickered, then caught my expression and shrugged. "A blood test and a five dollar license is all."

When she left with the menus and our orders, Norma called softly across the table: "Tom—"

I scowled into her eyes glowing at me and said thickly, "Call me Jack."

I was lost.

5

The horse-faced Justice of the Peace showed me the gap in his yellowed teeth. "It's customary to kiss the bride, Mr. Colby." His stout wife beamed. The other witness, his spinsterish daughter, simpered. Norma Colby, née Peters, turned a flushed face up to the Jack Colby I had become. Her eyes were blurs, her lips dry and motionless.

Portents.

In the almost ten hour drive to the Appalachian foothill town of Hampton, her face remained flushed, her eyes blurred, her lips motionless. She sat as far away from me on the seat as possible—as if the civil ceremony had somehow erected a barrier between us, as if we had been married forty years, pieces of domestic furniture content to do little more than vegetate side by side, as if everything we could have said to each other had already been said ten thousand times before.

Actually, I could not bring myself to talk.

She would not.

Hampton turned out to be somewhat smaller than Midville or Thurston City, but a lot more attractively situated, nestling alongside a swiftly rushing stream, surrounded on all sides by wooded slopes. That time of the evening street lights were on and the main street, through which the highway brought us, was ablaze with neon. I spotted four movie houses, several restaurants, a scattering of bars, two small department stores, a Sears and assorted other shops.

About ten miles past Hampton, most of it uphill, Norma finally spoke: "There it is."

A slowly rotating neon sign high over the four-lane black-top: ROBSON'S MOTEL. Below that, a stationary smaller neon sign: VACANCIES. I could barely make out the unlighted: NO in front of the vacancies sign.

I pulled up on the highway's shoulder short of the motel. From there we could see a slender blond man servicing a Toyota at one of the three pumps.

"Hobson?" I asked.

Her head shook. "Mr. Hobson is a much older man. There's a driveway circling the house, with a sort of carport for us in the back."

The house was stucco, with dark wood trim, giving it a sort of rustic appearance. The second floor overhung the pumps. On each side of the house I could make out the same decor on the cabins set back among tall pines. Floodlights illuminated the whole setup. Across the road, just beyond a low concrete wall, ran a deep ravine flanked by tall tree-clad slopes. Beyond the ravine I could make out distant peaks. The air was balsamy and balmy.

"Nice," I said.

Norma nodded. "I fell in love with it at first sight. Tom, we'd better—"

"Okay."

I drove along the shoulder until it became the filling station's cement apron. I passed the pumps, then turned around the house on a gravel driveway, coming to a halt behind a loaded Buick station wagon.

As if on cue, a grey-haired man emerged from a rear door. Norma went out to meet him. He was saying, "Mrs. Colby! How nice to see you again! I'd almost given up expectin' you today. This Mr. Colby?"

He was almost as tall as me, with a craggy face and a grip that was surprisingly strong. I nodded.

"I'm Colby."

"Eric Hobson." He gestured toward the station wagon. "I've been packed and ready to take off all day." Turning to Norma: "The upstairs is all cleaned and waitin' for you, Mrs. Colby."

She said, "Jack, will you take the bags up, then let Mr. Hobson show you around? I've already seen it all."

I put one bag under my left arm, gripped the other two by their handles and followed Hobson into the building. Just inside the rear door a stairway ran up to the apartment, depositing us in a small foyer that opened on the living room. Dutifully, I let the old man show me the bedroom with its queen-sized bed, the kitchen equipped with, among other trivia, a dishwasher and freezer, and a bathroom with a tub I might sit in, but little else. Fortunately, there was a shower head over the tub.

Then I followed him down another stairway into the glass-fronted office presided over by a slender brunette in coveralls who was in the act of assigning a portly couple to one of the cabins. Hobson touched her shoulder.

"Helen, this is Jack Colby. He's buyin' me out."

Her hair was wrapped in braids around a neat, almost plain face. Her eyes barely flickered at my appearance.

"Colby, this is Helen Riley. She and her husband Bill outside have been practically running the place."

She put a cool hand into mine, gave me a tight smile, then turned back to the couple. I watched her reach for a key from the rack alongside her counter, then turned to see Hobson regarding me shrewdly from under bushy grey brows.

"You seem itchy to locate somethin', the way you keep lookin' around."

I grinned at him. "Your books."

They were in a tall metal filing cabinet alongside a cluttered desk in the rear of the office. Hobson cleared a space for me on the desk. I settled into the ancient swivel chair and riffled through the pages of the five ledgers. It was a ridiculously simple accounting system which, if accurately maintained, showed a business worth over half a million going for less than half its value. I glanced up at Robson's rueful smile.

"If I didn't need the money in such a hurry, Mr. Colby—"

I waited for more, but that was it. He then took me outside to inspect one of the unoccupied cabins.

I had seen more luxurious ones on the wrestling tour, but none neater or cleaner. Each had twin beds with firm innerspring mattresses and what seemed to be solid oak bureau-desks, night stands, armchairs and floor lamps. The light beige carpeting seemed new and freshly vacuumed. The light gold bed covers and tan blankets folded neatly at the foot of each bed seemed equally new. The bathroom, featuring a glass-enclosed stall shower, held thick white towels. It took a few seconds, but the hot water ran hot. Inside, the reading lamps, radio, and color TV all worked fine.

"No complaints," I told Robson's rueful expression.

He led me back to the office where we found Norma and Helen Riley going over the cabin registration procedures. Norma broke off to tell me, "Jack, why don't you go outside and get the feel of the pumps while I wind things up with Mr. Hobson." Correctly interpreting my expression, she said, "Oh, don't be so macho, darling. I'm much more familiar with the details and we'll save so much time—"

I shrugged and wandered out to where the lean blond fellow was holding a Visa Card out to the driver of a maroon Cutlass Supreme. The Cutlass drove off and the young fellow turned—almost into me. His eyes jumped. I grinned at him. "Don't let my size throw you. I'm your new boss. Jack Colby," and held out my hand, which he took, grinning at me.

"Bill Riley. You a football player?"

"Was. Does my size bother you?"

Riley's grin widened. "Hell, no! It'll come in handy Saturday nights, when the kids come horsin' around. Some Saturdays they're almost more'n Hank and me can handle."

"Who's Hank?"

"Works here weekends, when traffic picks up."

"What's he do the rest of the week?"

"He goes to Hampton High. Except Summers, of course. Then he fills in for Helen's and my vacations."

I nodded. "Okay, Bill. I'll pitch in when it gets heavy, but you'll have to show me the ropes. I never pumped gas before."

The lesson began almost immediately, as a beat-up station wagon loaded with children pulled up to the regular gas pump. Before the Chevy pulled out, two more cars had nosed in off the highway. I had to learn on the run. How to check oil and water levels, and tire pressures. There were the restrooms around the side of the building to be pointed out. There was the business of imprinting credit card slips —after first checking their authenticity on the weekly warning notices. And the cars kept creeping in off the highway. After a while I grew aware of Eric Hobson standing behind me.

"You'd think I arranged this to impress you," he said wryly. "But it's been gradually building up like this over the past year, Mostly it's been like this weekends—"

Norma emerged from the office, her flaming hair encased in a dark green scarf, the remainder of her lost in olive drag coveralls. "My turn to learn the pumps, darling. You can work with Helen on cabin registrations—after, that is, you sign the last few papers for Mr. Hobson."

My signature was needed on such items as transfers of the corporate bank account, the Hobson Motel, Inc. stock, and one final document absolving Eric Hobson of any responsibility for claims or lawsuits against the corporation originating after that date.

Hobson shook hands all around, then drove off in his Buick station wagon; figuring on getting at least a hundred miles behind him before stopping for the night.

I had difficulty concentrating on what Helen Riley was telling me, most of my concentration on what would transpire when the Rileys left.

Things began to slow down outside about ten. Norma went up to the apartment first. The last cabin was rented ten-thirty. Helen showed me the switch to light the NO in front of VACANCIES. By eleven, Bill showed me how to lock the pumps, shut off the floodlights and turn the OPEN sign behind the glass office door around to read CLOSED.

The Rileys drove off in an ancient Ford Mustang.

I locked the office door from within, put out the office

lights. I should have been exhausted. My feet seemed to grow wings going up the stairway.

Under its closed door, I could see the bedroom light was on. I spent ten minutes in the bathroom soaping the grease and sweat off me and showering, then toweled myself briskly, wrapped the towel around my midriff and entered the bedroom.

Norma's knuckles were screaming at me.

She sat in the beige-upholstered easy chair, the scarf off her flaming mane, but the dark green coveralls still on and buttoned up to her neck, her white-knuckled fists pressed into her stomach as if it ached.

Her voice was strained: "Tom—"

"Jack," I said.

"We haven't had a chance to talk."

"I'm listening."

Her flush deepened. "This morning I was... weak—"

"Rebounding from shock," I said, frozen in the doorway.

"Yes. And I—we—"

"Got natural," I supplied.

"Rebounding from shock, as you said," she said, her face almost as red as her hair. "You may have assumed we'd continue—" Her fists opened into hands gesturing helplessly. "We did agree it was to be a business arrangement, Tom."

"Jack."

"Jack. In spite of how we may have felt or acted this morning. Basically a business arrangement, if we should happen to fall in love, all right. But—"

I said, "Come here, Norma."

"What?"

"I want you to come over here where I'm standing. I promise not to touch you."

She came slowly—until about a yard separated her flushed face from the scowl I was unable to keep off mine.

"Look at me," I said. "I mean, really look at me!"

"Tom—"

"Jack," I said, taking the step that put my face almost directly over hers. Her eyes clung to my neck. I said, "I could use the couch in the living room. I've slept on worse. Any way you want it. It's a damn good business arrangement. We could sell this place tomorrow and net over a quarter of a million profit. So that's not the point. Whether it is your prudery or my face is something I have to know. Damn it, look at me!"

When her eyes reached mine, I knew.

I whirled out of there, slamming the door behind me—and discovered the couch had already been converted to a bed.

I flicked off the reading lamp and lay awake most of the night, thinking of her in the queen-sized bed, remembering the electric delight of her nakedness against mine, the excitement of her tongue dueling with mine, feeling the icy snake slowly slithering around the linings of my guts.

6

It was not until I was on my breakfast coffee that she put a hand on my shoulder and leaned close to look squarely into my eyes.

"Listen," she said, "it's a chip on your shoulder. I've looked at you before without knocking it off—just as I'm looking at you now. It's when you challenge me, You get such a terrible expression. It's frightening. And when my fright shows, it enrages you—knocks that chip right off—"

"Awakens the snake in my belly," I cut in.

"What?"

"An image that came to me as a kid. When I first learned how girls reacted to me. I walked half the night feeling something cold and slimy coiling itself through my insides and thought of it as a snake. That's how I think of it whenever—"

"When you feel people are trying to shove you into a cage?"

I nodded dumbly.

She leaned even closer, touching her lips softly to mine, then drawing back, smiling. "See how it can be when the chip is off your shoulder. There is so much to like about you. Give us both a chance, Tom—Jack. I can't just crawl into bed with you—not you or any man. Not so quickly. You have to build up to it. Help me."

"How?"

"Don't try forcing me."

"Okay."

"Woo me."

"How?"

"However you've wooed girls before."

I shook my head.

"Never?"

I shook my head again.

"Well, make it up. Remember I have feelings too. Invent ways. Be nice to me, the way you really are inside. When your niceness shows, I like you. Just keep being nice to me. Okay?"

"Okay."

And that wound healed.

Danny Baker entered my life a week later.

Bill Riley, the usual grin off his freckled face, told me, "Feller in cabin nine wants to see you, Mr. Colby."

I nodded and walked toward the cabins thinking of my week of wooery. There really had not been much time, what with the business eating up most of my daylight hours. There was the need to supervise the three women who came out on the bus from Hampton to clean the cabins in preparation for the next day's occupancy, and the need to maintain an endless stock of supplies for both the cabins and service station. This on top of pitching in at the pumps and registering guests. It took sixteen hours of each day, leaving only eight for sleep and whatever. "Whatever" involved getting Helen Riley to bring back from Hampton such items as flowers, perfumes, costume jewelry and whatever she thought might please Norma. Another part of "whatever" developed when I learned Norma enjoyed my reading poetry to her. She said my voice was like the low notes of a cello.

Such obscure poets as Eliot, Pound, and Joyce were too abstruse for her. How she put it, "If I was into puzzles I'd rather do crosswords." She loved Marvel's "To His Coy Mistress," and other romantics such as Lovelace, Byron, Keats, and Shelley.

Seven days that had shimmered by like seven seconds.

Now I rapped on the door of cabin nine and a man's voice called that the door was open and to come in. I came in.

The man sprawled on one of the twin beds, a fat cigar in his plump face, a man about forty, with reddish hair, small grey eyes and soft lips around the unlit cigar. He wore a pale blue shirt over grey trousers that was carefully tailored to accommodate his bulging midsection. From the bathroom came the sound of the shower in operation. My gaze moved from the woman's black dress and black underthings on the unoccupied twin bed to the man, whose jacket lay neatly folded beside him.

"I'm Danny Baker," the man said in a hoarse voice. "You Colby?"

The radio was on to a newscast. Someone named Anderson was still at large despite a three state dragnet in which federal authorities assisted. I went to turn it off, then nodded at the man. "I'm Colby."

He was frowning up at me. "You know, there's somethin'

familiar about you. Got any idea where we coulda met before?"

"What do you want, Mr. Baker?"

"It'll come back to me," he said. "What I got's a proposition right up your alley. Good money in it for everybody. We can—"

He broke off as the bathroom door opened and a blonde came into the room toweling herself. Her eyes were small, but her mouth, breasts and hips were large. Her waist was surprisingly slender.

"Mabel," Danny Baker said past his cigar, watching me from the corners of his eyes, "this is Mr. Colby. He owns the place."

Her eyes took a lazy inventory.

"Gawd! Ain't you a big one!" She showed me her excellent teeth. "Wanna dry me off, goodlookin'?"

I watched Baker remove the cigar and study it. "Mabel's the proposition, Colby. Her an' four more like her. They got a regular clientele from maybe a hundred miles around. Twenty-five to fifty bucks a go, an' they go all night, non-stop."

Mabel slowly hip-walked almost into me, only the towel between us. "Daytimes I'd be sleepin' here, Big Man," she drawled in a husky voice. "Raw. I sleep raw. But there's this about me; I hate t'sleep alone. It drives me crazy." The towel flicked away and all of her became warm and soft against me. She husked: "I go crazier not sleepin' alone, you big, hard man!"

Beyond her, Baker spoke lazily. "It'll be worth fifty to you a night. For each of five cabins. That's two-fifty every single night—all year round. Seventeen-fifty every single week. Ninety-one grand a year. Cold cash under the table. Which puts it right up your alley—hey, Colby?"

I breathed, "Why up my alley?"

Baker regarded me slyly. "It ain't no secret, pal, how word

gets around Hampton. I know Hobson drove outta here with two hundred and fifty grand in cold cash. Nobody deals like that unless it came to him under the table in the first place."

I was only dimly aware of the blonde's hands on my shoulders while she leaned back to give her center of gravity leverage against mine, her voice a husky purr: "You an' me, you great big hunk! We'd go through a bed a week!"

My palm wedged between her out-thrust breasts.

"Don't shove me off!" she panted, lost in her swaying, grinding dance against me. "I'm gettin' ready to pop! Hold me tight, tight, tight—"

My palm flicked.

She flew back across the beige broadloom into Baker, who was coming off his bed, yelling, "Hey!"

The snake in my belly was alive and out of control.

Baker got free of Mabel and came up yanking at his hip pocket.

I helped get it out. A small black automatic. Then I had it and Baker was cowering back into Mabel, holding his fat palms up toward me. "Now wait a minute, Colby. If I made a mistake—"

The snake was in my throat, my voice, hissing: "Out!"

Baker tried again, torturing the cigar in his mouth. "Just listen a minute, Colby—"

"Danny, don't!" Mabel cried hoarsely. "Look at his eyes!"

I went to the door and kicked it open.

"You getting out?"

"For Gawd's sake!" Mabel screamed, "Lemme get a dress on!"

I could stand no more: not her, not him, not the snake spinning through my guts.

Baker grabbed his jacket and, for all his bulk, swiftly darted past me toward the Cadillac parked outside.

Mabel was trying to wriggle into her black satin dress. It

caught on one jutting breast. I stepped past her, gathered up her underthings and black pumps, gripped a handful of her blonde hair and dragged her, stooped over like that, out the door, more out of her dress than in.

Baker had the Cadillac's motor purring and the door open for her. I tumbled her in beside him, tossed her underthings and pumps on top of her, slammed the door and stepped back as the big car's wheels spun the gravel of the driveway, then caught and lurched out to the highway. It crossed, whirled with a squeal of tires and brakes, then zoomed off toward Hampton.

I scowled down at the little automatic in my hand, then flung it across the highway and into the ravine beyond. Bill Riley appeared at my elbow, his freckled grin restored.

"I woulda quit," he said through it. "Not now. I'm right proud to work for you, Mr. Colby."

I asked, "Hobson let people like that use the cabins?"

"Deacon Hobson? Nobody in his right mind woulda tried. He wouldn't even allow cigarette machines in the office."

Further conversation had to be tabled. A line up of cars summoned us to the pumps where Helen Riley was stooped under the raised hood of a Mustang, checking its oil. I could see Norma in the office, registering a young couple with two children. I joined Bill at the pumps and, an hour later, when the action slowed, asked him:

"Why'd Hobson sell out for so little, Bill? The way I figure it, he could have collected at least double what we paid for it."

"Not up front, Mr. Colby. He needed it up front. His missus had bad lung trouble."

"I see."

"He'd sent her to Arizona an' kept tryin' to sell out an' go join her. But everyone wanted to lay down a small deposit an' pay the rest outta income. Mr. Hobson couldn't do that because he'd arranged to buy a big motel outside of Phoenix, an' they hadda have almost a quarter of a million up front. It looked real hopeless until you folks came along."

I nodded, forcing my expression and voice to remain non-committal.

"Okay, Bill. We understand one thing now. No whores get to work out of these cabins."

"That's exactly how I like it, Mr. Colby!"

I remained outside at the pumps until the Rileys were gone. Then I turned on the NO sign, locked the pumps, turned out the floods, locked the office door behind me and turned off the office lights.

This time each step up to the apartment was an alp.

7

Norma was still up. Trusting me now, she was sitting up in the queen-sized bed, propped by pillows, wearing her black lace robe over nothing but herself, her brows puckered over Eliot's *The Waste Land*.

"Honest, Jack, this makes absolutely no sense to me at all. Listen to this—" Glancing up at me, her thought died. "Jack, is something wrong?"

I crossed the carpet to brood down at her alarmed expression, unable to keep the rage out of my voice: "Where was it?"

"Where was what?"

"Not the diamond bullshit. The two hundred thousand grand you paid old Hobson. You probably got it out of the car while he was showing me around, then gave it to him after sweet-talking me to go out with Bill and learn the pumps. Where was it hid?"

She began turning away, was stopped by my fingers grabbing a handful of her coppery locks, holding her head rigid.

"Jack! You're hurting me!"

"Just tell me where you hid it."

"In the spare tire," she barely breathed.

"How?"

"It was flat when—" Her breath caught. Shock flooded her eyes. My grip kept her face angled up toward mine.

"When Colby tossed the money to you? When he came running out of the Midville bank with it?"

"Yes," she whispered. "You're hurting me!"

"Just look at it as the way a sucker woos. Is that how Colby really died? Shot down outside the bank while you drove off with the money?"

"I didn't know then that he'd been shot."

"How'd you manage to pump up that tire with all that loot in it?"

"This gas bomb Jack had given me—"

"Goff and Sinclair. They were the two who'd gotten away?"

"Yes."

"And that's what they were after? The money?"

"Yes."

So there it was. Finally. I released her hair and watched her face drop into her palms. I said, "Colby had this motel deal figured out as a hideaway after he double-crossed them, didn't he?"

"I don't know," she mumbled through her palms. "Most likely—"

"Most likely?"

She lifted shock-stunned eyes to me, her breasts pushing the black lace out, sucking it in. The panicked breathing of my dream girl, my wife, my nightmare.

"Yes! Yes! Yes!" she sobbed. "He was rotten! I loved him! I'd have died by his side gladly! But I didn't even know he'd been shot. He was supposed to come along in the Pontiac with Goff and Sinclair and Johnson. Johnson was the man who was shot down with him. We were all supposed to meet in the parking lot of a diner in Columbus, Ohio. But you're right. Actually, Jack intended to slip away from them at the first opportunity and make his way by bus to Hampton where he would meet me. He was going to marry me there, then come here and pay Mr. Hobson the two hundred thousand balance, and we'd—"

"Live happily ever after," I supplied. "The retired bank robber and his moll."

"I didn't know he'd been shot," she went on, as if I had not spoken, "until after I had pumped up the spare tire on a back street in Midville. When I got behind the wheel I turned on the car radio—and there it was. I could tell from the descriptions it was Jack and Johnson who'd been shot dead. I must have fainted—"

"Must have?"

"I'm not sure. It was as if I closed my eyes for a moment, then opened them. The radio was still on with the story. I couldn't think. All I felt was that I had to get away from Midville. I'd forgotten about the money, the motel, the baby. All that mattered was to get away. I felt numb, so numb I wasn't sure I could drive. At the first crossing I almost ran into an oncoming car. That's when I stopped for you."

I stared down at this beautiful wife of mine, this bandit's moll whose smile distracted a policeman long enough for her confederates to shoot him dead.

"You really did it!" I growled, scarcely aware of ripping the black lace robe free of her hands struggling to keep it wrapped tightly about her. "All my life I managed to steer clear of the cage," I told her panicked eyes as I finally got the robe loose and tossed it behind me. I began undoing my own clothing with one hand while the other and my weight kept her from squirming free. "But you dragged me in, baby! You lied and sweet-talked and cock-teased me in. And now that I'm this far,

I may as well go all the way! All the way, baby! Right up to the hilt!"

The cage became a darkness alive with fists beating at my face and fingernails clawing my arms... It became lips writhing away from mine... It became a sleek torso writhing and twisting to get from under me. Where the only sounds were my hoarse breathing and her gasps—

It became a breathless moment when my knees pried apart her thighs, and the very core of me thrust, plunged, corkscrewed into a soft, warm, moist nest—

It became rigidity under my thrusts—gradually melting into a matching rhythm as lips flamed into mine and reached for my shoulder blades to pull me down tighter and tighter toward the very core of her.

It became an exquisitely torturous series of crescendoing blasts that echoed and re-echoed down the corridors of my spine.

It became sleep.

8

A finger of early morning sunlight stroked the cascade of coppery silk on her pillow, crept gradually down to caress the soft curve of her back. She heard me stirring and spoke dully, facing away.

"Now what?"

I touched the sunbeam on her back. Her skin seemed to shrivel under my touch. I brooded down at the back of my long, thick finger.

"Don't," she whispered, hastily adding, "please?"

"Not the chip on my shoulder," I said. "Not what you see in my eyes. It's the rest of what's around my eyes. My face."

She whispered, "Yes."

Like dreading to open a telegram, fearing bad news, then

opening it and finding the news worse than bad—horrible. I withdrew my finger and said, "I don't know what."

"I tried," she whispered to the wall. "I honestly tried to fall in love with you. There's so much about you I genuinely like. And then I needed you so desperately."

"You needed a sucker. And there I stood with my ape face hanging out and my thumb in the air."

"Not like that, Tom. None of it was planned. One thing simply led to another. It wasn't cold-blooded. Things just happened—and I had to improvise as I went along."

"How'd you meet Colby?"

"At a bowling alley In Santa Cruz. I fell in love just looking at him bowling. Tall. And dark-haired, with little dabs of grey at the temples. And a lean tanned face. And his eyes—when he first looked at me my knees actually trembled. I'd read of girls reacting like that but never believed it could really happen. Two weeks later I left Santa Cruz with him. Quit a good job, emptied my bank account and gave it all to him. Almost fourteen thousand dollars. By the time I learned he made a living robbing banks I loved him too much to care."

"There's twenty-thousand still unaccounted for."

"In the kitchen. Behind the refrigerator. I didn't know what to do with it. Do you want it?"

"I want to figure a way of sending it back without it getting traced back to here."

She turned and got up on an elbow to face me. "Does that mean you'll—we'll—keep on?"

"I don't know."

"I could keep trying, Tom. For a while last night—in the darkness—it was almost as if I did love you. In the midst of all your violence you became so tender—and at the same time so excitingly strong."

I crawled off the bed and stood scowling down at her.

Adam and Eve confronting one another's nakedness without any reactions at all.

I said, "Helen, Bill and the cleaning ladies are almost due. I'd better go down and open up."

"All right, Tom, but—"

"Jack," I said

"Jack. What about us?"

I studied the gentle rise and fall of her breasts. "There's this about us," finally came out of me. "I don't think I can keep going on with just a daytime wife."

Her breasts stopped. Everything stopped: the sun, the tides, my breathing. She finally said, "I'll try, Tom—Jack. I promise I'll try. At night—when it's dark—"

And the snake in my belly lunged.

9

That hour of the morning I had the bar to myself. And a lonesome bartender whose efforts to launch a conversation came apart against my expression; that scowl glowering back at me from the blue-tinted mirror behind the bar as I broke my lifelong abstinence and tasted rye. Gloversburg. Three hundred miles northeast of Hampton, in the next state; a large enough city to have street corner mailboxes. Twenty thousand dollars in two hundred bills inside a manila envelope clumsily addressed to the Midville bank in a script my left hand barely managed had gone into one.

The remaining two hundred thousand? We could try selling the motel and sending in anonymous payments as we got paid. There would be profit for us at the end of such a deal, the difference between two hundred thousand and whatever we could sell the motel for. But that wouldn't be realized until after the first two hundred thousand had been paid, probably a matter of ten or more years. How would we survive until then? Assuming Norma would even consider such a drawn-out arrangement.

Capable of looking at my face and kissing me gently, yet terrified at my slightest advance. Beauty and the Beast, with no magic transformation in sight.

The rye burned my throat—but it could not soften my memory. *I promise to try. At night—when it's dark—*

My glass was empty. The bartender waddled over with the bottle and another conversational feeler. "Ain't it a hell of a note, this guy Anderson?"

A radio down the other end of the bar was blaring a newscast, the same I seemed to have been hearing off and on for over a week, about a man named Anderson still being at large.

"What's the note?"

"Comin' to life in the morgue like that. Back in Midville. And then bustin' outta the hospital after killin' a second cop. That'll be eighty-five cents."

"Who was the first cop?" I breathed.

"Ain't you been readin' the papers?"

"I've been out of touch. Too busy."

"One of them guys stuck up the Midville bank an' got shot down outside. Then came to life in the morgue. They had him in the hospital under guard—until somehow he got this other cop's gun away an' killed him with it. Been raisin' hell all over the place since."

"You sure that was his name? Anderson?"

"Sure I'm sure."

"Where's your local paper printed?"

"The Gloversburg Sentinel?"

"That's it."

"Down the Sentinel Building. Down Main and Fourth. Like I was saying—"

He was saying it to my departing back.

They let me scan two weeks of back numbers—and among them I found "Anderson" on a front page. There was a picture of his "body" sprawled on the sidewalk outside the Midville bank. There were police photos from prior convictions, showing him full-face and profile. There was a listing of his aliases—and among them was "Jack Colby."

As Norma had described him. Lean, greying temples, with deep brooding eyes.

He had served time for armed robbery in Illinois and Kansas, and was out on parole after serving three of twelve years for an Oklahoma bank robbery. He was thirty-nine, six feet tall, a hundred and seventy-three pounds and considered, according to one prison psychiatrist, to be a "psychopathic personality." The public was warned not to attempt his capture, but to notify the nearest police authority if he was spotted.

In subsequent editions of the Sentinel, the Midville coroner surmised the shock of being shot had stilled "Anderson's" heart long enough for the first doctor on the scene to pronounce him "dead." An X-Ray taken in the hospital disclosed that the bullet had lodged between two ribs, leading to the additional surmise that it had been a ricochet, accounting for its failure to actually kill him. The patrolman guarding him in the hospital had been found inside "Anderson's" room, his head smashed, presumably by the officer's own revolver, which was missing, along with his uniform.

A traveling shoe salesman had been stopped by a uniformed patrolman on the highway a few miles south of Midville. Ordered to leave the car, a Pontiac Phoenix, the salesman was struck down. He awoke in some shrubbery off the road, his clothes and the car gone. The abandoned uniform was found a day later by members of a Boy Scout troop out on a camping trip in another patch of shrubbery just a few hundred yards from where the shoe salesman recovered consciousness. The Pontiac Phoenix was found two days later in Thurston City.

A few hours before the car was found, a hardware store was robbed in broad daylight—two blocks from where the car was found. The store's owner was discovered by a customer on the floor behind his counter, beaten to death by a "blunt instrument," the contents of his register, estimated to be no more than sixty dollars, was missing, as well as his wallet, car keys and car, a Honda station wagon.

After that, the stories reduced themselves to: HUNT FOR ANDERSON WIDENS, and THREE STATE DRAGNET, and ANDERSON STILL AT LARGE.

It took four and a half hours, breaking speed limits most of the way, before I pulled up to the spot on the road's shoulder from which I had first studied the motel. It seemed to be basking in the usual late afternoon lull, Bill Riley fussing around the super snleaded pump and nobody else in sight.

Which signified nothing. Where else would Colby be headed? He knew Norma had the bank loot. The plan had been to meet her in Hampton, then finalize the deal for the motel.

He could have been here ten hours after knocking off the hardware store in Thurston City, could have lurked in the woods surrounding the motel days ago. Could have scouted Hampton and learned of the "Colbys" who had bought out Eric Hobson. Could have lurked in the woods and seen Norma, seen me.

Then what?

More to the point, what was my move? Apprise the State

Police of his probable advent? Sensible, but stupid, That would tie me right in with the bank holdup—simply by having purchased the motel with the bank loot.

What else? Keep on the lookout for him and capture him when he showed?

Just as stupid. In the first place, I was not equipped to single-handedly pull off such a cops-and-robbers ambush; in the second, if I handed him over to the authorities, wouldn't that land me behind the same complicity eight ball?

I had one final alternative, assuming he held off exposing himself for a while, which seemed reasonable, since his problem was even more complex. He had to figure out a way of recovering Norma and recovering the bank loot, now embodied in the motel, possibly by assuming possession of the motel—without drawing dangerous attention to himself. Assuming it would take a little time for him to work this out in his mind, I could always spirit Norma away from there, the two of us settling in some hideaway in another state, and from there negotiate sale of the motel long distance, through intermediaries Colby was in no position to trace.

Settling for that, I nosed forward and onto the cement apron, drove around the house and parked in the rear. Rather than go upstairs immediately, I went into the office, where Helen Riley told me: "Mrs. Colby asked for you to be quiet when you go up. She wanted to sleep. Said she wasn't feeling well."

I nodded, asked, "Anybody interesting register?"

"So far, nothing but tourists," she said.

Examining the register, I noted they were all couples. It was unlikely Colby would come to Norma with a woman.

"I'll go up and check her out," I told Helen, then mounted the stairs wondering how—or if—I should bring up Colby's resurrection. And how I should broach the subject of a quick move to another state, settling in under aliases and trying to negotiate sale of the motel long distance.

Reaching the apartment, Norma called out, "That you, Tom?"

"You're supposed to be sleeping,"

"I tried, but I couldn't. You want to come here for a moment?"

From the bedroom doorway, I was too confused by what she was doing to continue my train of thought. Her back was to me. She was laying out her dresses on the bed. Alongside her, on the carpet, were her open suitcases.

"You said you'd try to make a go of it," I breathed.

Her back stiffened. "I honestly meant what I said, Tom. But then, thinking it over—"

"What?" I demanded, stepping into the bedroom.

"I changed my mind."

"I changed her mind!" a man's voice said bitterly from my left.

Whirling, I saw him seated in the big armchair with an automatic pistol in his right hand pointing at me, in a blue suit too large for his lean body, and the face paler and more gaunt than it had appeared in the news photo. His lips were twisted as bitterly as his voice.

"I change things," he said.

"Like a fungus!" I heard myself growl, unable to keep from lurching toward the black automatic rising toward me. It had a peculiarly long barrel. "Everything you touch," I heard myself, "rots and dies!"

"Like you!" he said, and that peculiar end of the automatic seemed to explode into a scarlet blossom and my right leg was no longer under me.

The bedroom carpet was under me, pushing into my face, filling my mouth with the taste of grit.

But no noise from the shot. It bothered me. Just a mechanical click.

From off to my right I could hear Norma saying, "You promised not to hurt him." From behind me a man's voice said: "Finish the ugly bastard!"

Goff or Sinclair, I thought, feeling bewildered that I did not really know which was which, but suddenly realizing why the click: that peculiar extension of the automatic's barrel must have been a silencer.

Hearing Colby's bitter voice: "Not yet, Einstein. How's he gonna sign all those papers if I finish him?"

And a third man's voice: "Watch out! He's still comin' at you!"

Sinclair or Goff, I thought, realizing I had been almost reflexively crawling on one knee and two hands, dragging my right leg, trying to focus on Colby's saturnine face through a gathering pink fog.

"You stop him!" I heard Colby's voice. "He's cut down to your size now!"

Legs appeared between Colby's face and my eyes, and I heard a sound like fists hammering on a distant door. Looking up, I glimpsed the greyed bulldog-faced man who had been gripping Norma's head back in that first motel, and the dark-haired man who had been applying the flame of the cigarette lighter to her feet. Sinclair and Goff. It bothered me that I did not know which was which. Both had patches of tape on their heads and faces. The dark-haired one's right hand was completely encased in bandage, leaving only his left free to grip the blackjack beating down on me, while Bulldog Face used his right to piston his.

Was Norma screaming? I seemed to hear Norma screaming. Even when my head seemed to split open to admit the exploding grenade and my whole world became a crescendoing series of blasts I seemed to hear Norma screaming, screaming...

10

Thousands upon thousands of sharp little pins were jabbing into my arms. My left leg throbbed. MY right leg felt numb. My head entertained one long, endless, pulsating ache. I tried licking my lips but could not muster sufficient saliva. I grew dimly aware of hands tugging at my wrists, and Colby's bitter voice: "You idiots shoulda thought of that before. Suppose his writin' hand's paralyzed?"

"You said tie him tight," one of the men I had heard before protested.

"Okay. Goff, I'm not faultin' you—"

Which made the bulldog-faced man Goff. The one whose hand I crushed would have been unable to tie knots. I felt fingers toying with my right eyelid.

"Want me to snap him out of it, Colby?"

"Not until Norma cans those Rileys. How about it, Pimp. You got replacements for 'em?"

"I wish you wouldn't keep callin' me that."

Danny Baker's voice.

"You'll be wishin' a lot more when it comes time to slip the blade into him."

"Count me outta that!"

"It's too late, Baker. You're too far in. After we get your fifty G deposit, how do we insure your payments for the rest? You'll be sittin' here packin' it in with whores in half the cabins, while we'll be out there in the cold waitin'. So it's insurance. Your hand on the knife, your prints on the handle —and the ugly bastard planted where you don't know. Stop the payments, we'll blow and tip the cops where to dig him up and whose prints match those on the knife they'll find still in him. Blow the whistle on us, same deal. So it's gotta be you, see?"

"Suppose his wife don't wanna deal? It takes both their signatures."

"She'll do exactly like I say. Which reminds me—she ain't to know we're gonna ice the Ape. When it's all wrapped up, she'll drive off with me. The fellas will take care of him after we're gone. In the meantime, no word about this where she can hear. Got that?"

"I never killed anybody in my whole life."

"Get used to the idea."

"I'm gonna be sick—"

A rasping sound, followed by Colby's laughter followed me into a dark silence. When the darkness ebbed, I heard Norma saying: "...see why we have to include Goff and Sinclair. After what they were doing to me—"

"Want a lift, hon?"

"No. It just doesn't seem fair!"

Sound of a liquid gurgle, followed by, "It breaks even, hon. You ran out on them with the dough. They tried to get it back. So it's squared, and we start all over again. Sure you can talk Ape into signing all those papers?"

"When I explain how you'll let him go—" There an uncertain pause while I tried flexing my fingers behind my back. The needling sensation was gone. Blood was circulating freely through my arms once more. I could feel a rope binding my wrists fairly loosely. My head continued to ache.

My right leg felt bloated, numbed. I tried pulling my hands free of the rope, could not—but my fingers were able to reach a knot. They began working it, as Norma asked, "Jack? You're not lying to me—about letting Tom go after he signs?"

"What's the matter, hon—he grow on you?"

"In a way."

"What way?"

"He's sensitive, and—"

"That gorilla?"

"You'd be surprised, Jack. And inside he's very decent."

"Yeah? What am I like inside?"

"Rotten."

I could hear Colby laugh. "If I didn't show up, you mighta gone for him all the way, huh?"

A long pause as my frantic fingers finally began unraveling the knot. Then, hesitantly, "I don't think so, Jack."

"Because of how he is on the outside?"

Another pause, as I finally worked my wrists free of the knot and reached carefully for the rope binding my ankles, then: "Yes."

"So it's the outside that wins out, huh?"

"Yes, darling."

"Like mine, huh?"

"It's all I ever wanted, darling."

"So—" his voice got smoky "—why waste it, hon?"

Sound of bedsprings, followed by Norma's: "Jack, no! Not with all those men outside the door!"

"They'll stay until I call 'em, hon. Whaddya think's been on my mind from the minute I woke up in that goddam morgue?"

The bedsprings again.

My eyes snapped open. I lay on the beige carpet, wedged between the bureau and the wall, with my head far enough past the bureau for me to be able to see their legs, trousered and nyloned, dangling off the bed. As I watched, Colby's hand slid up her skirt, then swept down her right leg carrying her stocking and shoe before it. They dropped to the rug.

I found the knot on the rope binding my ankles and began tugging at it with fingers of both hands as Colby's hand rode down her left thigh, this time, carrying her flimsy black lace garter belt, as well as the stocking and shoe before it to join the other stocking and shoe on the carpet.

This was a much tighter knot, but I could feel the strength

pouring back into my fingers with each passing second and, finally, it began to give as I watched Norma's dress, then her bra and panties join the other items on the carpet.

Then Colby's shoes, followed by his ill-fitting blue trousers, his white shirts, his briefs.

Then Norma's, "Oh, darling!" moan.

And Colby's hoarse: "Honey-sweet, I been thinkin' a nothin' but this every goddam minute—"

The bedsprings took over rhythmically as the knot binding my ankles finally came free and my fingers clawed at the needle pricks stinging my left ankle, trying to force circulation back into that foot. My right was hopelessly numb and useless. And through the rhythm I heard Colby swear, "You'll never get away from me again!"

And Norma gasped, "Never!"

And then I could hear no more. My own heart was smashing too loudly in my ears. But I felt them. I could feel them through the floor. Them and the snake writhing wildly through my belly, lunging, squirming, twisting, crawling—

Later, I was unable to recall how long I stood propped on my left leg, gripping the bureau's side, looking down at them.

My wife and her bandit lover. The wide patch of bandage over his chest pressed her breasts almost flat beneath him. Their mouths were sealed together. Sweat streamed from the short hairs on Colby's nape, down his back into the bandage. They seemed to be moving in slow motion. Norma's eyes were closed. My wife. My harlot wife. My nightmare—

Becoming her nightmare, as my first hop brought me halfway across the broadloom toward them. As I teetered, gathering balance for the hop that would put them in reach of my hands, her eyes fluttered halfway open, began closing, snapped wide.

Her scream erupted in his mouth. Colby tore himself around and, for the instant it took to complete my second hop, four eyes seemed to be screaming at me to crawl back into my cage.

The snake in my belly was going berserk. My balance was leaving.

I could see Colby's hand leap to the neck of a half-filled bottle of Jack Daniels. I could see him raise it, then smash its bottom down on the edge of the oak nightstand. I could see it swing up at me as I finally dove.

Whiskey, blood, and shattered glass streamed down my face. My ears vibrated from the sheer terror in Norma's screaming. I was vaguely aware of my hands catching Colby's chest bandage, enabling me to pull him close as the jagged bottom of the bottle leaped again at my face.

But my face was numbed. As through a red fog I watched my hands forsake the bandage for a grip on Colby's throat, felt them tighten, felt something crack—

From behind me a babble of male voices, and then again that sound like fists hammering on a distant door. *Not again!* raged through my mind, and I crumpled to my knees on the carpet, twisting about. I caught a foggy glimpse of legs. I shot my left arm out to scythe a broad arc through the legs, buckling them, bringing their owners down to where I could see their eyes, their horror-struck eyes begging me to crawl back into a cage, telling me who I was, screaming the story of my life with their eyes.

I had Colby in reach, and Goff, and Sinclair, and Danny Baker, and even Norma—all merging into a single pair of terrified, blood-soaked eyes—

It was as if they kept disappearing and then popping up again, like targets in a shooting gallery, forcing me to slash at them again and again and again—until my arms were leaden, until a whirlpool seemed to form under me, sucking me down. I fought it, but its tug was too strong.

My knees spun into it, then my hips, then my chest, finally my head.

And all became blackness.

~

Bill Riley found us. Six motionless, blood-drenched figures sprawled on and off the bed. Only Norma and I still alive.

It was a bit more than four months before the Hampton Hospital released me. My right leg would have a permanent limp. Plastic surgery had restored my face to what it had been before the mêlée. I declined the surgeon's offer of what he called "beautification."

My return of the Midville bank's twenty thousand, plus my return of an additional sixty thousand for the assorted rewards for capturing Colby, Sinclair and Goff, plus the manifest worth of the Motel, induced the powers that be at the Midville bank to settle for a twenty year mortgage covering the balance still due them.

The Larson Motel now, twenty-five percent of which is currently owned by the Rileys in appreciation of their successful operation of it during my four months, plus, in the hospital.

It took Norma another two months before she could leave the hospital. Long before then, a miscarriage had eliminated Colby's child. She happens to be carrying mine at this writing. It was nip and tuck for a while before the Midville authorities decided not to prosecute her for her lesser role in the bank robbery. They took what happened to her under consideration.

Her conversion to absolute love for me, began with my hospital visitations and increases to this very day. She lives, she tells me, for the moments I spend with her, especially when I read to her.

Her clinging dependence becomes, occasionally, a bit much. She has mastered Braille, but still would rather hear the words in my "cello-like voice."

One subject we never discuss is Colby and the events of that fateful evening. She mentioned it only once, the day I brought her home from the hospital.

Her last memories were of Colby gripping the neck of that Jack Daniels bottle and swinging it wildly from side to side. That, she knew, was how the jagged glass of the broken bottom ripped the sight from her eyes.

Nobody told her—nor will they—nor will I—that Colby's and Goff's and Sinclair's and Danny Baker's eyes had *all* been slashed by the jagged ends of that bottle.

Or that Bill Riley found me sprawled half over her, with the bottle's neck gripped in my fist.

Tight.

So tight that it took two men to pry it loose.

9 781966 037606